THE ONES WHO STAYED

SHANNON ST. HILAIRE

WILD SAGE

Contents

THE WALLS

2016

Agnes wants to sit on her bench, the one under the mango tree. She wants it with a deep, twisting feeling inside her that she tells herself is just back pain. With a few minutes to spare before she needs to leave, she changes into a floral top and her brightest white pants to match her hair, and heads out to the garden.

But the volunteer from the States is there, lounging on the bench, carefree, careless. The girl should know it is Agnes's bench, though the girl has no knowledge of the memories infused in every object, even the adobe walls of this house. Agnes swallows the desire to say anything about the bench to the girl because she isn't supposed to have possessions. That is one vow she upholds, at least in her actions if not her thoughts.

She doesn't have time to be sitting around anyway. She always has places to go. Because if she isn't careful, if she's idle, the walls whisper. They wake her up with shadowy nightmares she can never remember. They chase her out of the house. These walls, which she has repainted every two years in the same shades of yellow and green, know all the things that happened here, thirty years ago.

CHAPTER 1

THE MESSENGER

1986

The young man's head had been freshly severed when they put it on the spike. Blood dyed the wood dark red and then pooled below, turning the grass into a black swamp.

Yes, his face was frozen in terror. But what struck her was the blankness of it. The permanent blankness, shouting how wrong this was.

His name was Miguel and he was twenty years old. She had known him almost since she arrived in this place, before he joined the FMLN as a guerrillero. He came to Mass every week with his mother, Tatiana, and his three brothers and two sisters.

That was why she was here, in this park. As a sister, neutral and benign, neither side would attack her. Only she could tread upon the land dedicated as a place of terror and leave unscathed. Only she knew to whom the head belonged, and only she could bring it home. This was her fifth such errand in her time here. Five heads in five years.

The first time, a more tenured sister, Helen, had seen

the head on the spike and come home to fetch her. Agnes was then initiated into one of her many duties. The first man had been older, in his thirties, his long hair tied back. His face was preserved in her mind. His name was Rutilio.

Helen had left just last month, after her seventh head, and the other sisters could not bring themselves to take over this task. They would have left the head to drip and decay in the afternoon heat. Agnes would not allow such a thing. So, when a boy knocked on the door that morning to tell what he had seen in the park, it was Agnes who acted, on her own for the first time.

Soldiers loitered at the edge of the brown lawn, smoking cigarettes and eyeing her. They were not allowed to harm her but that was not always enough to stop them. She could feel their young men's desire for violence trained on her. For all she knew, it was these same soldiers, boys really, who had done this to Miguel last night, and now they were enjoying the sight of the American nun cleaning up. Townspeople slunk by, trying to see what was happening but too afraid to stop.

She performed the sign of the cross and said a silent prayer, for peace for Miguel, for strength for herself. Then she pushed back the sleeves of her habit and, with a white sheet, used both hands to grab his head and pry it off the stake, gently as she could. She would not gag or vomit or cry, would not take any more dignity away from him. Then they would win. The head slid off, and she wrapped it in the sheet. Holding the head in front of her but not against her, arms already beginning to ache, she closed in on herself so the soldiers would not see any reaction, would be disappointed that they were not getting a show. She could not do this but it had to be done, so she would do it as someone other than herself, as the messenger.

Agnes walked back to the truck she'd borrowed from the clergy house. She placed the head in the passenger seat and drove toward the barrio where Miguel's mother lived, monitoring the package in her periphery to ensure it was not jostled. In the distance, bullets rattled off. Sometimes they were just warnings, and sometimes they were not.

As she drove she thought of Tatiana, whose life she would soon change forever. Tatiana was quick to scold, not just her children, but anyone. Agnes had tried to teach her to knit once because Tatiana claimed she didn't know how, and then a few weeks later she had produced a knitted purse with a zipper and a handle and Agnes's name embroidered on it—something Agnes herself would not have known how to make and certainly had not taught the woman. That had been years ago, and Agnes recalled laughing with Tatiana and bending down—being taller than most women, especially in this country—to kiss her on the cheek in thanks. Tatiana had replied with her typical Vaya pues, the Salvadoran version of you're welcome, a self-deprecating Go on then.

The sound of the shots grew louder as she approached the barrio. She pulled over, the familiar sensation of her body's instincts taking over as she identified the risks. Ears perked, eyes unblinking, heart beating. How keen her senses had gotten in the last few years.

The popcorn sound of the bullets, then an explosion. They were far enough away, she decided. She could not do this later; there was nothing she could do with a head that seemed reasonable, and to keep Tatiana waiting any longer would be wrong.

Agnes put the truck back in gear and kept going. Her hands on the steering wheel looked like someone else's.

. . .

Outside Tatiana's home, powdered debris rained from the sky. Whatever action was happening was not on this street, but that could change at any moment.

When Agnes lifted her hand to knock, she saw that it was stained with blood. She clenched it into a fist and knocked with the knuckles that were only marked by her own freckles—too many, the doctor said. Irish skin wasn't meant for the Central American sun, but what could she do.

She knocked again. Behind the door, Tatiana told the children to stay down, stay away. Spanish reprimands rattling off a harried tongue.

Tatiana, short and round, with the slightest lines forming on her face, answered the door, wearing a soiled apron. Buenas, Hermana Agnes, she said, beckoning Agnes inside. Pásale, pásale—

Tatiana's eyes traveled down to the bundle in Agnes's arms and stopped there. Blood had leached through the sheet in places. Agnes wanted to cover up the spots but it was too late. Tatiana would already know.

I have to tell you something, Agnes said.

Tatiana was frozen, but Agnes ushered her into her house, closing the door behind her. Tatiana's other children, none more than ten years old, peered from the next room with wide eyes. Agnes closed the curtain that separated the two rooms and returned to Tatiana, who hovered in the corner of the room farthest from her children.

It's about Miguel, Agnes said, and rested a hand on Tatiana's shoulder, remembering too late that there was blood on it.

I am sorry, Agnes continued. I found him this morning and I am bringing him back to you.

Tatiana slumped against the wall, eyes still locked on the

bundle in Agnes's arms. Then she snatched it, unwrapped it, and fell to the ground, clutching her son's head close to her. The chaos of mortar and collapsing buildings did nothing to keep the children from hearing the wails that racked the cement floor beneath their feet, the stucco walls of the house, Agnes's own bones.

Agnes could never do enough. She felt herself retreat, floating away, away from Tatiana's cries. The shell of her remained, holding Tatiana.

The first time, Agnes had asked Sister Helen if it were not better for the mothers and wives and families not to see the heads. Helen had explained the importance of the physical to Salvadoran culture, how close they lived, how much they touched, how they were buried next to one another. In the last decades, so many were simply disappeared, and their families searched for them tirelessly, often without success. She told Agnes that so much had been taken from these people, they had no right to withhold anything more. Besides, Helen had tried it, and the mothers and wives always begged to see what remained, did not believe her unless they saw the proof, touched it. Agnes only wished that there had been someone else, someone besides her, who could have gone ahead and given Tatiana the news first.

Eventually, Tatiana's eldest son came home. Rafael, all gangly limbs he had not yet grown into, stood in the door-way. He asked, Mami, ¿Qué pasó?

He crouched down next to Tatiana, saw his brother's head cradled in her lap. His face contorted with grief, but he gathered up Tatiana in his arms and rocked her gently as she buried her face in his shirt.

You are the man of the house now, Tatiana said, her voice muffled.

Agnes helped Tatiana stand, and wrapped up the head so the children wouldn't see. Agnes made corn coffee and sat with Tatiana as she somehow composed herself to tell the children. Tatiana held Miguel, what was left of him, the whole time, whispering, Dios me ayude. Behind the curtain, the children were silent.

At home, Agnes slipped off her habit, which she only wore for tasks like these, her own version of armor. It reeked of blood and tears and terror. She would have thrown the habit away, if she could. But that would be frivolous, an act of emotion, not of practicality, when she could not easily acquire another habit, when it could be cut into strips for bandages.

The numbness, which had been a reprieve, was drifting away. In its place, anger filled Agnes and hardened inside her. Tatiana, who was good and kind, who thought she could not knit, was not able to fight. So Agnes would.

She did not think about the last time she spoke to her parents all those years ago, that clipped phone call in which she'd chastised them for running late, that day she had left the country.

She filled the stone basin with water and soap, and scrubbed the habit until her fingers were raw, until Sister Margaret came home and gently pried the brush out of her hands.

CHAPTER 2

UNDER THE MANGO TREE

She went out to the small garden shared by the convent and the clergy house often, to the bench under the mango tree, to pretend for a moment that there was peace. As the rainy season approached, she watched the small green oblong shapes grow and grow and turn to red and orange and yellow as if there were still life in this place. She imagined they grew in size before her eyes over the course of a sunset, perhaps even fueled by her gaze. In turn, they filled her with hope, provided her with oxygen as she provided them with carbon. Symbiosis in a land torn apart.

The garden was cocooned in trees and bushes, and beyond lay the artificial lake, built years ago to be a source of electricity. It was the only place to be shielded, at least partially, from the constant noise, not just of bombings and commands and cries, but of the chatter of her four beloved Sisters of Charity, of the neighbors' voices from the connected house next door leeching through the open space between the walls and the ceilings. Everywhere noise, everywhere smells, everywhere people.

She sighed, this the only moment she ever exhaled.

Exhaled the shrapnel buried in the arms of children, the tears of mothers cradling broken bodies, young girls' fear as they became women in the mountains.

On this evening, she was out the back door and halfway across the garden when she stopped.

Someone was there. On the bench, a place only she ever went.

And it was too late to go back inside because the collared man on the bench was turning to look at her. She had never seen him before. She forced the corners of her mouth upward.

He returned her smile and scooted over on the bench so there was room for two.

She would have to keep thinking in and speaking Spanish, despite the weariness of that part of her mind after a day's use. After five years, she had more or less all the vocabulary she needed to express herself, but it grew harder to access the words as day turned to night. Perhaps there would be small talk, which was easier but more tedious— yes, it was hot and humid today, as were all days this time of year—or a more sophisticated conversation in which her broken sentences and unrolled *r*'s would be on display. It was all she could do to prevent her shoulders from hunching over, from revealing the weariness she hid everywhere but here, as she walked the rest of the way to the bench and sat down. She would not exhale today, and the thought was a weight that rested on her chest.

Good evening, said the priest.

He spoke English, easily it seemed, from the way the words had rolled off his tongue. Agnes sank into the seat next to him. She could exhale after all.

He told her his name was Raúl and she replied that hers was Agnes. As often happened, they discussed her patron saint, the twelve-year-old girl whose hair miraculously grew to cover her naked body as she was paraded through the streets, a punishment for refusing to marry.

No, Agnes said when he asked, she had not chosen this saint to be hers when she took her vows; rather her parents had chosen it for her, and she had kept it.

It is always nice when things work out so beautifully, he said.

She nodded, although she disagreed. He saw, and asked.

She said she kept the name because she did not want to bother with choosing a new one, but she disliked the reason St. Agnes's story became well known. Her chastity was a commodity men fought for and which she died to preserve, all because of her beauty. A plain woman would have been sent to a convent or killed without a note of it in history, without the recognition of sainthood. The entire story was premised upon her beauty and her purity, things that shouldn't matter, all while she was still a child.

And the miracles she brought forth, he said. Flames did not touch her when they attempted to burn her at the stake. Men who tried to violate her were struck blind; one was struck dead until she prayed for him to be revived.

To this, she agreed. It was nice to discuss miracles, something other than war and death. They both looked out onto the black ripples of the lake. The breeze played on their faces.

How long have you been here? she asked.

I transferred from San Salvador last month, he said. He told her he'd lived his entire life there until then. He needed to be somewhere less visible than the capital, although it was becoming more difficult to go unnoticed by the junta.

Images flashed through her mind, of the priests who had already been martyred, of the assassination of Archbishop Óscar Romero, hero to the poor, as he led Mass at the beginning of the war. The American nuns like her who were picked up at the airport, violated, and murdered by soldiers in 1980, just a few months before Agnes had arrived, flying into that same airport. Still, those deaths were seen as the outliers; members of religious orders, particularly nuns, were usually seen as immune, harmless, invisible.

What brings you here? he asked. This is not a place most Americans would choose to be.

She explained that she had lived in Massachusetts her whole life until she came here in '81. She had taken her vows four years prior and the Mother Superior could tell she was already restless, itching to do more—so she sent Agnes to El Salvador.

I got to choose the town, and this one has a classical music station, she said.

I, too, enjoy that music station, but it is not much basis for a choice, he said.

I could have asked for another assignment, but I read the teachings of Monseñor Romero, and wanted to continue that work, she said. I don't know that I am doing anything of the sort, but there is certainly much to do here, with no end in sight.

She did not usually talk so much about herself, but it was such a relief to speak English, to speak frankly to someone other than the sisters she lived with, that the words rushed out. Still, she held back some. She did not mention her parents, what had happened to them.

How did you come to know English so well? she asked.

From my studies in Canada, he said. It has been quite useful over the years.

He traced the shape of the small, brown book in his lap. The edges were worn, as if he did this often. The cover of the book faced down, his hand covered the spine.

He resumed the conversation, saying, I can tell from the long hours you spend away from here and from the burden on your shoulders that you do far more than anyone should have to do.

How do you know any of that? she asked, too blunt.

He turned his gaze, looked at her with warm brown eyes.

I'm not as dense as I may seem, he said, almost smiling. I notice things that happen around here. You come here, to this tree, for peace. I have disturbed it and now I will go, but if you ever want to talk to someone who will listen, I am just next door, and that is what I do.

He rose, holding the small prayer book—no, a book on liberation theology—against his stomach, where it clinked on the cross that hung around his neck. She had scared him away with the bitterness on her tongue.

Thank you, Padre, she said.

She looked down because inexplicably her eyes burned. But she never cried anymore, not in front of people. As his footsteps retreated, she wondered, Why did he hide from the military; why had he read a book until its cover was worn smooth, yet seemed to hide it from her; how had he managed to reveal nothing about himself while she spoke so much about herself?

CHAPTER 3

FAMILIAR WORDS

At night, alongside her sisters in a row of cots, Agnes lay awake, hearing the brushing of the bushes in the garden, faraway voices that echoed through the walls. Despite the heat and the unbearable humidity, Agnes pulled the blankets close around her.

For no reason at all, when she had finally almost fallen asleep, she'd jolted awake with the memory of her parents, standing over her, their backs rigid. She was ten years old, and hadn't raised enough during the Knights of Columbus fundraiser. She'd had a cold, hadn't felt up to going door-to-door in the middle of a New England winter. There was no excuse for staying in bed all day, they said. She had so much, and others had so little. Out they'd sent her to shovel the snow on their neighbors' driveways until her fingers were stiff from cold.

She clenched her hands, open, closed; her fingers were not frozen, they were slick with sweat. Still, she was wide awake after that memory, so she prayed. She would deny till the day she died that the prayers no longer meant anything, hadn't since her second year here when the violence she had witnessed accumulated in her bones until they overpowered her feelings of faith. But the rhythm of the familiar words, which she knew as well as her own name, were a comfort long after they'd lost all meaning. She knew they were true even though she could no longer feel it and she would follow them wherever she was meant to go. That was her penance. Because if the words weren't true, there would be nothing to save her from the whispers in the night, from the horrors that awaited in the day.

When she went to the mango tree now, she almost hoped he would be there. Maybe he thought he'd bothered her— she certainly had thought he would—but she found she did not want to be alone, even when she went there to be alone. For weeks he did not come. She would not go to him—a sister would not simply knock on the door of the clergy house just to say hello.

And then, one evening, he was there. He read from a prayer book and looked up as she approached.

I hope you don't mind, he said. There are few places to find solitude.

I don't mind, she said, and sat next to him.

They gazed upon the mango tree, its long leaves dewy. Padre Raúl rose, taller than most Salvadoran men—she estimated that he was almost exactly her height. He lifted a hand, rustled among the foliage, plucked a fruit.

The first mango of the season, he said, and offered it to her. For you and your sisters.

We should give it to the children, she said.

It is for you to do with as you wish, he said.

He still held out the mango, and she took it from him.

She rolled its weight between her palms, ran her fingers over the leathery, supple skin. It was a warm yellow, perfect in its ripeness.

Things still grow here, she said, trying to understand how it could be.

Shall we pray together and give thanks, Sister? he said.

They took out their rosaries. Agnes paused.

In Spanish? she asked.

Si lo deseas, he said.

Agnes listened to her own voice weaving together with his deeper one. With a faint pang, what she used to call homesickness, she recalled how, as a child, she and her family had prayed the rosary every night, clustered around a small table with a single burning candle. It had felt so simple, so certain. Her parents, her brother, and Agnes each thumbed their own rosary. Hers, with cream-colored beads, had been blessed by the pope—a First Communion gift from her uncle, who was a priest and had studied in Rome. It was the same rosary she prayed with now, its beads slightly darker from years of use. She used to wish they would change color completely as she prayed, a miracle that sometimes happened to the truly faithful. But hers never had, and that was how she had known she was not yet good enough. For some reason, she wanted to tell Padre Raúl about that childhood memory, but it seemed a foolish story given the times. The simplicity felt like a lie now. Nothing was simple.

They prayed on until the Hail, Holy Queen—Ea, pues, Señora, abogada nuestra: vuelve a nosotros esos tus ojos misericordiosos—beseeching mercy that never seemed to arrive. With an amén, they concluded their prayers. Her eyes met the priest's, and she read her own thoughts in his eyes. Prayer was not enough. They would find their own mercy.

The next day, when she took the mango along with other food to the neighborhood school, she smelled the wrongness first: a sharp, metallic tang in the air. A crowd was gathering in front of the school—adults shepherding the children away, people approaching, then standing silently before the gates.

Hanging from the bars were several mangled bodies. A statement. There was to be no learning here, no safety. Agnes remained standing in front of the gates, the mango a dead weight in her palms, and stared at the bodies.

She overheard a woman saying that the American nuns who ran the school were already on their way out of the country. The school was closed indefinitely. Of course, this had been the soldiers' intention—to drive away the helpers. And despite everything, the terror, the torture, the murder of civilians, the United States continued to provide aid to the Salvadoran military. One million, sometimes two million dollars a day.

Her hands mashed the mango into a sticky pulp.

She stared at the bodies, because they made her angry, and anger was power.

The next time Agnes returned to the mango tree, he was not there, and she sat.

She thought of what had happened in the last few days,

since the school had closed. While assembling care packages, Sister Margaret had dropped a package of dried milk. The white powder exploded on their feet, a waste. Agnes had then snapped at Margaret, who was by far the most dimwitted and rattled of all the sisters in the house, and brought her to tears. Agnes had no patience for incompetence or nervous temperaments when there was so much to be done.

If any of the sisters left, no one would be sent in her stead. This had become a place of leaving; two of her own sisters had just announced they were going home, and Agnes knew the others would soon follow. It was becoming too difficult to pretend that it was safe here for members of religious orders. Soon she would be the last sister left, the only one who could do what she did, and she would not be extracted, no matter how her Mother Superior back home pleaded with her. She would never be able to return to a place where she'd been useless, destructive even.

The memory rose then, with perfect clarity, of the day she left for El Salvador. She had waited, bags packed, in the convent lobby for her parents to take her to lunch, to say goodbye. But they were running late, they always were. Agnes used to think it was their only flaw in an otherwise godlike existence.

Agnes had gone to the phone at the front desk and called them. Her mother had answered, in a frenzy of making muffins, rolls, and loaves for a bake sale. Agnes had rushed her mother, told her she had to go to the airport soon, she was calling a cab. Her mother had said, no, wait, they were on their way. Agnes could practically hear the flour poofing out of her mother's apron as she patted it. In the background, her father wondered aloud where his boots were.

You're leaving now, right? Hurry, Agnes had said, then hung up.

She waited a little while longer, then took a cab to the airport. She did not find out until after she arrived in El Salvador that there had been a car accident.

After six years, she could still hear the screeching metal, smell the burning tires, see her parents' terrified faces, as if she had been there.

She squeezed her eyes shut. She pushed down guilt, that paralyzing emotion; there was nothing for her in the States, the place of its origin. She would not return if there was even a slight possibility that she could help here. So she redirected her thoughts, to the weakness and violence of others.

He came out of the clergy house and to the mango tree as if responding to her silent request, and she confessed the blame she felt for the sisters who left in fear and the unholy anger boiling in her veins, and he absolved her.

So it went the next night, and the one after.

***

It was Sunday morning after a makeshift Mass in the square, and Padre Raúl was in her kitchen, teaching her to make pupusas the way his mother made them. As they had walked home together, trailing behind the gaggle of Agnes's sisters, he said every Salvadoran must know how to make them. Agnes, though never a cook, had agreed to learn. Masa, curtido, beans, fresh cheese, and loroco were scattered across the table.

What kind of pupusa do you like best? he asked her as they cooked beans and stirred masa.

Loroco, because I imagine it is slightly healthy, she said.

He chuckled at that—fried masa, crisped and dripping

with oil, was anything but healthy, even if there was a little green flower in it. She carried on as if she had not noticed; she wanted to keep this one delusion.

But I also liked chicharrón as a treat. And you? she asked.

Frijol y queso; I am a traditionalist. My mother used to make them for breakfast sometimes. Not the best way to start the day—we always regretted it—but delicious.

He showed her how to roll up the masa into a perfect ball, then press it flat, and into the center put beans and cheese. Then she was meant to close it up, encasing the beans and cheese with masa and pressing it into a flat circle once again. Agnes found the feel of the dough in her palm soothing and satisfying, but her pupusa came out in oddly shaped, oozing masses, while Padre Raúl's was a perfect circle.

He laughed—actually laughed out loud, from the belly; who could do that anymore?—at her egregious failure. He cupped his hands over hers to show her how to flatten the dough without breaking it.

A sister peered in to find out when lunch would be ready and his hands left hers with the faint flutter of a bird's wings taking flight.

MINUSCULE TASKS

Padre Raúl drove the truck while Agnes sat in the passenger seat. It was not often one priest and one nun ventured out into the world together, but these were not normal times. He normally made this journey with one of his brothers, but they were stretched thin these days, and she had offered to help.

They were on their way to the mountain to deliver supplies to the people hiding there. It had been only the guerrilleros at first, but now entire villages had retreated into the lands they knew so much better than the military —their one advantage, their one chance to stay alive.

The people in the mountains only trusted certain members of the Church with their whereabouts. Perhaps they wouldn't have told anyone, but then there would have been no one to bring them food and essentials. Six years into the war, they had already hunted the animals on the mountain nearly to extinction.

Padre Raúl and Agnes were bringing beans, masa, medical supplies, soap. The items required to sustain human life. Agnes often thought of what it would be like to be a woman in the mountains. It was uncomfortable enough, that monthly visitation, without having to use leaves as sanitary napkins and wait weeks or months to have the safety and water supply to bathe, particularly now, in the dry season. Combine that with a constant fear for one's life . . . bringing the supplies was the least they could do.

They trundled past bombed-out buildings and debris that reeked of rubber and hair and other things not meant to be burned. The streets were almost empty; most of the villagers of the province had evacuated to the mountains. They yielded to military vehicles and tried not to look at the faceless men with guns as big as their bodies. She wondered if any of them ever went to Confession, and what it would be like to hear their sins recounted. A helmet tipped up, metal glinting in the sun, and she saw: a young face, still marked with acne, with dark eyes that looked much older. She averted her eyes and noticed, tucked in the console, the same book of liberation theology Padre Raúl had been reading the night they met. She considered asking him about it, but she did not wish to confuse the religious with the political. Her calling was to care for people, not to fight.

As the cobblestone road turned to dirt, he revealed that he was an avid bird-watcher. He pointed out exotic birds as he saw them, slowing the truck to a crawl.

El Torogoz, he whispered reverently. Our national bird. See its turquoise tail?

Agnes did not see, but pretended she did because he was delighted. How a person could be delighted in this world was beyond her, but he was, and it was a balm to be near it. She had become distant from these emotions. Looking back, she realized she had not felt anything like delight in a year, or perhaps two. She could not remember, exactly, when those kinds of things had stopped happening.

It took hours on the bumpy, winding roads to make it to their designated meeting spot at the foot of the volcano Guazapa. As it was still early in the rainy season, the mountain was brown and seemingly devoid of life, but surrounded in the haze of humidity. The truck ground and crunched to a halt. Then silence. Not even a bird chirped.

Agnes strained her eyes, scanning the woods Lito and his men should emerge from, to exchange a grateful handshake and haul up the goods. Agnes quirked her eyebrow at Padre Raúl with a silent question to which he shook his head. They should be here by now.

After a time, he opened the door of the truck and got out.

I have to find them, he said. If the men have not been able to make it to the meeting spot . . . any number of things could have prevented them. They may need my help.

Do you know where they are? she asked.

He nodded and did not explain how he knew. She did not ask, but got out of the truck, too. Padre Raúl held up a hand.

It's too dangerous, he said.

It's not too dangerous for you, she said, so it's not too dangerous for me.

She set off, hiking up the trail of the mountain. He soon caught up with her, and wordlessly they began to climb.

They walked together for an hour, perhaps two, Padre Raúl guiding the way to the civilian camp. Agnes wished she had worn something more durable than a skirt that went down to her calves and sandals that exposed her feet to every twig and thorn.

Why did you come to El Salvador? Padre Raúl finally asked in a low voice, hopefully low enough to avoid detection. She knew conversation, about anything, would distract from the fear that silence brewed.

There was a need, she said.

There is need everywhere, he said. Why this need?

It is our fault.

Whose?

America's. We are funding this war, these atrocities. I joined my order because it is one of action, of social justice. When I was asked to come here, I felt the call from thousands of miles away. I had to do something to counter the blind injustice of my country.

Hermana Agnes, you are not them. You do not need to carry the weight of what your government is doing. You are here, helping.

Agnes did not answer, did not try to say she was guilty so that he would console her. They walked on in silence for a few moments.

Did you know it would be like this? he asked.

I could not possibly have imagined how hard it would be, she said. Perhaps a foolish side of me thought I would fix things, save people. I was young and inexperienced then. But it is better that I did not know—I would not have had the strength to come. Now I know that it is the tiny, minuscule tasks that are all most of us can do, and we must all try our best, and all added up together, maybe something good will come of it someday.

Why don't you go back? Things are only getting worse, and you could escape all this.

Agnes's insides clenched from stomach to throat.

This hardship is all that is real, she said. I have learned that I am stronger than most. I have the benefit of my health, a good education, and few personal attachments. In the face of horror, I fight instead of running away. I have discovered that almost everyone else runs.

Bien, Padre Raúl said; the faintest smile perked the corners of his lips.

You could leave, too, go to Spain or Italy perhaps, and be safe, she said.

He shook his head, the smile fading.

I could not, less than you could, he said. This is my home. I am doing work here, work that no one else alive is doing, and right now if I left, no one else could do it.

Agnes chewed on the words, but did not ask what that work was. Sometimes it was better, safer for everyone, not to know.

We could never leave, she said, because this town has a classical music station.

His smile returned. They discussed the merits of Vivaldi and Debussy for a welcome few minutes until the conversation lulled.

What if you could do more than minuscule tasks? he asked into the silence.

It would depend on what you mean, she said.

What do you know of liberation theology? he asked.

Before she could answer, military shouts and the stomping of boots sounded in the distance. Soldiers were approaching; this must have been the threat that prevented the men from meeting them. Padre Raúl and Agnes ducked off the path and into the bushes. They exchanged a glance, mouths shut. Agnes's heart beat loud in her chest. To be found assisting the guerrilla movement would be their death warrant.

After an eternity, the noise faded and they rose, joints creaking. They resumed their climb, but did not speak again. After holding her breath for so many moments,

Agnes found she was having trouble remembering how to breathe properly. Breaths came in short spurts, which she tried not to let him see or hear.

When they arrived at the spot where Padre Raúl said the community had last made camp, there was nothing but a clearing with benches, hammocks, a firepit, metate, and comal for tortillas. The camp had been abandoned. This was not the site of a massacre.

The corners of Padre Raúl's mouth turned down in concern; he had not been notified that the community would be on the move, which meant that they had fled. But they had done so neatly. Padre Raúl and Agnes surveyed the ground for signs of where they might have gone, to track them. He set off in a direction, and Agnes followed. Along the path, the chichipince and chipilín shrubs were missing their leaves, harvested for their healing properties.

Agnes heard a faint *psst*.

Her eyes snapped toward the sound and saw a pair of black eyes peeking out, just above the ground. She closed the distance with several steps and crouched down.

Get in, the owner of the eyes said. Rápido rápido.

He lifted the lid, disguised by branches, so they could climb into the hole in the ground. The tatú entrance was completely dark—no way to tell what else was in there. The man, small and spry, stepped back to make room and the blackness swallowed him. Agnes was closest and should go next, but she hesitated. She could not see even a foot inside.

Agnes swallowed, her body revolting against what she must do. She wanted to turn and run back down the mountain, but it was too late for that.

Vení. The man's voice was a hiss.

She stopped thinking, turned off her instincts. She grabbed hold of the makeshift ladder and descended.

Freshly hatched spiders clustered around the entrance. She would not be able to react if any of them touched her, not only because it would betray her foreigner's fear, but because any sound could cost them all their lives.

The moist, dark walls closed in on her. The tunnel was not quite tall enough for her to stand, so she remained in a hunched position. Agnes glanced at Padre Raúl, who was right behind her. She stepped back to make room for him as he closed the lid and immersed them in darkness.

The man led them down the short passageway. Agnes's face was inches away from the rifle strapped to his back. They reached the main area of the tatú. The hole carved into the earth was meant to fit ten, but it was packed with what looked like thirty people who stared at her with wide eyes under the dim glow of a single flashlight.

There was a drop last night, the man whispered. There was a bomb raid to clear the ground, then helicopters dropped troops. We broke into small groups and have been hiding down here ever since. We do not think they have found anyone. You must stay with us until it is safe.

I'm Lito, by the way, was all he said as an introduction.

Hermana Agnes, she said, appreciating his bluntness.

She tried to fathom what was happening, silently, in this mountain. Padre Raúl had told her there were at least three hundred people in this one community. Could they really all be hiding in tatús, undetected? Yes, they could, because they had to. Her eyes flickered to a young woman holding a baby.

If only she had stayed at the truck, if she hadn't come out to the mountain today, if she had not come to El Salvador . . . But no, she had to do all those things. Those hard, dangerous things, because she was called to the people, could not give up on them. And now she would wait with them, below the feet of the soldiers who would torture, violate, and slowly kill them if they found them.

She looked at Padre Raúl, and he nodded. This was what they had to do and they would die with these people if necessary, without fear. She nodded back.

Lito clicked the flashlight off, and the darkness pressed in.

CHAPTER 5

QUIET

They'd been hiding for hours, or at least that was what Agnes suspected. With no watch or light to see it with, she had no way to track the passage of time. The air was stale with sweat and countless shallow human breaths. Once, Agnes adjusted her aching legs and pebbles crunched below her feet, causing Lito to glare at her, looking as if he would kill. She did not move after that. They took turns crouching and standing. They waited. For what, Agnes did not know, but she could not ask. Lito would know when it was safe, as if he were in tune with the mountain itself. At times they could hear the soldiers thundering through the forest, breaking branches and barking commands. They were oblivious to the entire community below their feet, their bodies becoming one with the earth.

Agnes caught herself regretting, again and again. She remembered sitting in the chair in her Mother Superior's office almost six years ago, fiddling with the fabric of her sleeve—she could barely sit still back then. Mother Josephine's stern eyes saw right through Agnes; she said she saw fortitude in her, and so she asked more from Agnes than she did of other sisters. The assignment was clear: Mother Josephine was asking her to walk into danger. Agnes had felt proud. Mother Josephine gave her time to decide.

Agnes remembered asking her mother for advice, using the one phone in the office of the convent. She played with the spiral cord as she told her mother, thinking she and her father would be sad or lonely or worried if Agnes left them and went to El Salvador. Instead, her mother had called it an honor, only asking Agnes if she was willing to die there. She'd considered that, too.

Agnes educated herself, read the news every day, with headlines such as "The Agony of El Salvador" and "In El Salvador, No Escape from the Horrors of War." Then she read "The Colonel," a poem by Carolyn Forché.

She closed her eyes, trying to remember how it went, the poem about the colonel who collected the ears of his victims in a jar. How he poured them out on the table and some of the ears fell to the floor, where they listened to his words mocking the rights of anyone.

After reading that, Agnes felt no doubt. Her only thought was that she didn't care for the heat, but she would get used to it.

At any point, Agnes could have, should have said no. Only a person suffering from insanity would have made the decision to come here.

It was time for the shift; Lito turned on the flashlight and those who were crouching stood, and those who were standing crouched. Agnes stood and pressed her back to the earthen wall.

She looked around at everyone, slowly, silently moving. The pain of remaining still and cramped for so long showed on their faces, but they said nothing. A jug of milk was passed around; everyone took one tiny sip. Agnes studied each of their faces. Lito, stoic and strong. The young mother, afraid but brave. Padre Raúl, wise and mysterious.

Them. She had come here for them, and would stay for them.

A few grains of dirt crumbled off and fell inside the collar of her shirt, but she couldn't move, so she ignored them.

Hours more passed. The soldiers wandered far from the tatú, and Lito allowed a few whispered words. The soldiers approached again, and he shushed them into silence.

And then, when the soldiers were closer than ever, close enough that they could hear boots cracking branches as they walked, the baby began to sniffle. The noise grew to a whimper which would quickly become a sob, and that could not happen. All Agnes could see was the panicked whites of so many eyes. The mother shushed and cooed and rocked the baby, increasingly frantic. Told her, Tranquila. Lito hissed commands. Be quiet, or leave the tatú. Beside Agnes, Padre Raúl radiated tension. The sharp stench of fear filled the air. Any moment the soldiers would hear.

There was no way to calm and quiet a baby trapped in a tatú, but still the mother tried, for countless moments they could not spare. Agnes cast about for something to help, but there was nothing. She was close, so she extended a finger for the baby to hold but she punched Agnes's hand away with a tiny fist. The baby's snuffling grew louder. Her mouth became a tiny O as she inhaled, preparing for a full-lunged wail. Before the breath was complete, the mother, tears streaming silently down her face, buried the baby's nose and mouth tight against her chest. Held the baby so close she could neither let out her cry nor take in another breath. The whites of the mother's eyes turned to Agnes, asking a question: Could she do this? Agnes swallowed once, and nodded. She reached out and gently laid her hand on the woman's shoulder, an attempt to let her know that she was not alone, and felt the woman's sobs as the soldiers' clumsy footsteps sounded above. The seconds ticked on, each moment one more in which the baby went without oxygen, until the seconds became minutes.

They could have sworn they heard something, the soldiers were saying, but now there was nothing. Their commander scolded them for wasting time circling back, and they marched on. As the pounding of their steps faded away, nothing was left but silence and the barely audible sobs as the mother unburied the child's face from her chest to find that she held only a tiny body.

Lito snatched the baby from her arms. He tilted the baby's head back and listened, then blew into the child's mouth once, and then again. People clustered around and he shooed them away.

Danos espacio, he ordered as he laid the baby on the ground and pressed the heel of his hands against her chest. A snapping sound, a break of the ribs. Agnes swallowed bile.

It was far too late. The baby was limp. Still, Padre Raúl tried, others tried, and the baby would not wake. Agnes heard whispers of horror, murmurs of prayer. Lito shushed them. Several people, not only the mother, were crying.

Agnes folded the woman into her arms, wondering how many more times she would hold a mother's loss.

•　•　•

Lito had been gone for hours. The last time he left the tatú, he brought back a stack of thick tortillas and orders to remain hidden. The tortillas had been finished long ago, but more than food, what Agnes wanted was news that the soldiers were gone and they could leave the tatú.

The air was tight. She was desperate to climb out, just so she could take a breath. Pure mountain air was just above their heads. She had never wanted out of anywhere this badly. Once, her hand brushed against the baby, back in her mother's arms, and the baby's flesh was already becoming cool. She shifted away, and the rough sleeve of Padre Raúl's shirt pressed against her arm.

It was nearly dawn when Lito finally returned. He pulled up the lid of the tatú and called down.

Vaya, you can come out now, he said.

They shook out their stiff muscles and made their way out of the tatú. Lito and Padre Raúl nearly carried the mother out. They lowered her to the ground and leaned her against a tree. Her curly hair sprang out from the braid that ended at her waist. Agnes, body protesting, kneeled beside the woman and asked her name.

Elisa, the woman whispered, not taking her eyes away from the baby's slackened face.

Elisa, you saved us, all of us, Agnes said. You saved Lito, Padre Raúl, me, all the other people here. We all owe you a debt we can never repay.

Nearby, someone scoffed. Agnes looked up. It was a man, older, with a graying mustache and a beard growing in. He must have stopped shaving when he left home for the mountains.

You think you have done a good thing? he spat out. Do you not love your child? Murderer of babies. There is no sin worse than that. I would have gladly died for the child. We should all have been willing to do so.

Cabál, someone muttered. Exactly right.

Where were you then, when all this was happening? Agnes said. I did not notice you trying to stop her.

That Lito wouldn't let us do anything, the man snarled. It's his fault.

Padre Raúl put an arm around the man's shoulder and walked him away, speaking in low tones. Agnes was relieved. He was more likely to listen to a priest than a nun, a man than a woman. She was more concerned with the mother anyway, and how she was going to live with the decision she had made.

Not far away, Lito was already shoveling a tiny grave, ignoring them. Elisa tore her eyes away from the baby and stared at him.

He does not need to do that, she said.

She shook her head and held the body closer to her.

Agnes held her hand over the child and said a brief prayer for the faithful departed: Que su alma y todas las almas de los fieles que han partido, por la misericordia de Dios, descansen en paz.

Then she sat with the woman, silent, and the other women came and sat with her, too. Above them, dawn broke.

CHAPTER 6

A ROAD NOT TO TREAD

Whatever Padre Raúl had said to the man had quieted him; his sentiments were now conveyed through the ugliness of his face and his crossed arms, which the others ignored. A woman set about gathering a fresh supply of leaves and roots. When she finished, she went to the bearded man and muttered in his ear. They conferred for some time, and, with a final nod from the man, they approached Lito.

La onda está así—we want you and that woman to leave us, the man said, extending a finger to point at Elisa.

You do? That's too bad, Lito said.

His voice was casual. He had just returned from filling his canteen from a stream and began administering sips to the group.

Padre Raúl and Agnes exchanged a look. Agnes approached, to stand between Lito and the two threatening mutiny.

She opened her mouth, not sure what she was going to say, but compelled to do something. Catholicism was clear on the subject: it was never permitted to take a life, not even if it saved others. It was not up to humans to decide who should live and who should die. But Catholicism had not accounted for this world. There was no line from the Bible or the Catechism that Agnes could draw upon. She wanted to scream that none of it made sense. But she could not be the one to lose control, not now. Agnes rolled her shoulders back and began to speak.

Compañeros, we have nothing right now if not each other, she began, stammering on the words for "each other"; she never knew when to say "cada uno" or "uno al otro," or if the person with whom she was speaking was from a region that would use an entirely different phrase. No matter what she said, someone always complimented her Spanish—a brazen lie—or perhaps hid a smile behind their hand. But no one smiled now.

We are living in a time of impossible decisions, she continued. None of us will escape with our innocence, but if we are going to keep ourselves alive, we must accept our guilt and learn to live with it. We must forgive ourselves when we have done our best, and pray that God forgives us, too. Most of all, we must trust those who have good intentions, and Lito's are the best of all of us. My faith is in him. And, please, be kind to Elisa, who has sacrificed everything for you, and pray that someday you will have a little bit of her strength.

She surveyed the people around her, unable to tell if what she had said mattered, their faces inscrutable. She had not been confident, she had not been inspired; her speech had certainly not stirred up such feelings in others. But she had spoken all the words she had. Lito was their leader and he would bring them together in a way she never could, because she would never truly understand their lives.

It was time for her to leave the mountain.

Lito had informed her and Padre Raúl that the soldiers

would surely have discovered the truck by now, so they would have to hike down the far side of the mountain, then walk back to town. Agnes asked about the supplies they had left behind in the truck—didn't they need them? Lito replied simply that they would manage.

Go, he said. There's nothing more you can do now.

Padre Raúl and Agnes said their goodbyes and imparted their final blessings. Agnes cast one last glance over the man and woman stirring up contempt, and Lito, who would keep them safe no matter what. But the mother was gone.

Where is Elisa? Agnes said.

The bearded man, hearing Agnes, pointed into the jungle.

Se fue, he said.

Agnes dropped her pack, took off in the direction he had pointed.

She ran. The figure of Elisa, walking straight and rigid, soon appeared between the trees. Agnes soon caught up to Elisa. The woman still carried the baby.

Where are you going? Agnes said.

Elisa did not answer. She looked as if she were not there, not inside her body. A walking corpse.

What you have been through is indescribably awful, Agnes said. Being alone is not going to make it better. It's important to be with people. Especially now. The others will come around, and Lito is on your side.

At the mention of Lito's name, Elisa let out an impatient huff, but said nothing else. Agnes, too, was out of words. So she walked with Elisa, and planned to do so for as long as it took.

They walked for hours. The muted sun overhead did not break through the clouds or the trees. Elisa seemed unaware of Agnes's presence.

Then a voice called her name, soft and sure. Agnes slowed—it was Padre Raúl, carrying both their packs and catching up to her.

What are you doing here? Have you been following us this whole time? Agnes said.

Agnes walked faster to make up the ground Elisa was gaining. He kept pace with her.

I would say we have both been following Elisa, he said. I waited as long as I could, but we have to go now. It is a long walk back to town and we must make it before curfew.

We can't leave Elisa out here on her own, Agnes said.

You have done your best, he said. You walked with her for half a day. If she does not want help, then we cannot help her. Try not to worry; she is of the mountain and will find her way.

Agnes cast a glance at Elisa, already beginning to disappear into the dense growth of trees and plants, then took her pack from Raúl.

She followed him down the far side of the mountain. They stopped once for water at a stream, splashing water on their faces, drinking from their cupped hands, and refilling their canteens.

When they emerged from the canopy of trees hours later, on the far side from home, the late afternoon sun broke through the ceiling of clouds to warm Agnes's face, and she stopped. The force within her that she used to go on, the strength she showed for others, was drained. *One never gets used to this war. It is too much to bear.* The words echoed in her mind as if they were someone else's.

Padre Raúl turned when her crunching footsteps went silent, in time to see her slump to the ground, a slow-motion collapse. He was at her side in a moment, and rather than holding her up, forcing her to stand, he gently guided her to the ground in his arms. Agnes was not crying; it felt like there was nothing inside her, merely a hollowness. There was no soul, no mind, no strength to stand.

Her head was against his chest. The part of her that knew who she was knew this physical contact between them was not allowed, but she had no room to care. She had been holding people for five years, doing nothing but that. And in that time, and for years before that, no one had held her. No one had known that she needed comfort. She had not known it herself. They sat in silence while she tried to find herself again, but she was nowhere to be seen. So he began talking, quiet words that created a path.

I've never told you the full story of how I came to be here, he said.

His breath was in her hair, his voice rumbled through her body. She listened.

I was there when Monseñor Romero was assassinated, he said. It was galvanizing for me, to say the least. There has always been an unspoken rule: that Mass is sacred, that no violence can occur in that one place, for that one hour. And when the rule was broken, that was it for me. I began working with the guerrilleros, and I recruited two of my brothers from the seminary. We became priests together and continued our work. We spread the message of the Farabundo Martí National Liberation Front, of rights for the poor, and recruited members to the cause. We published articles in *Orientación* and we dared to write the word "justice"—that one word was all the military needed to start keeping an eye on us. They followed us everywhere. And then, one night, I suppose they thought they had proven our guilt, because soldiers hunted my brothers down as they left a clandestine meeting.

Against the top of her head, she felt his throat bob. He continued.

I should have gone to that meeting, but I had been summoned to perform the last rites for a dying woman. I was on my way to meet them afterward—instead I watched from behind a dumpster as they were forced into unmarked vehicles. Their bodies were discovered the next day.

Raúl took a breath. He shook slightly on the exhale.

Naturally they were looking for me next, he said. But even if I had not needed to flee, I could not have lived in that empty house without my brothers, walked past the spot where they were killed. I was the one who ignored the dangers. I pushed them to take risks with me. They might never have been found out if it were not for me. Every day since, I have tried to justify being the one who survived, to carry on the work for the three of us.

You mean you are still a leader of the guerrilla movement? she asked.

Fear for him chilled her veins.

Not a leader, he said. But I am one of them.

But you are always reading peacefully by the mango tree, she said. How can a revolutionary find any peace at all?

I follow where the Lord calls me, he said. He summoned me to the tree, and I went. And you were there. Perhaps He meant for us to meet. I have . . . not felt peace or stillness in many years. I have been all conflict and guilt and anger. And yet, the moment I saw you and the reverence with which you regarded that place, I began to feel calm.

He was holding her tight in his arms, and when he swallowed, she could feel a tremor, as if in anticipation. She leaned back to look at him. His hair had rumpled overnight; its waves were giving way to curls. He met her gaze. His eyes were solid and calm, yet bold. She saw that he knew what he wanted and was unafraid of it. She almost leaned forward, into him.

Rain began to fall, the first timid drops of the season.

With a jerk, she sat up, away from him. This was going down a road they could not tread.

I only meant to tell you that I want to help you find peace, the way you have helped me, he said.

She nodded and averted her eyes, and they both stood. His expression was unchanged, unruffled by her sudden movements. He was still confident, still looking at her. He asked her if she was feeling better and she nodded again. They walked on.

My sisters are going to leave, sometime soon, she said. I will be the last one in the house.

You will not be alone, he said. I will be next door.

CHAPTER 7

THE WORK

Weeks passed, and Agnes toiled. She set up a makeshift school in the ruins of the bombed-out church so the children could continue to learn. There were only five students, but it did not matter. She walked alongside known members of the guerrilla movement so they would not disappear. She used money from the Church to buy enormous amounts of food and took it to the poorest families, who increased in numbers by the day as employment plummeted and inflation soared. These families always invited her in and pressed little bits of handmade jewelry into her hands and fed her pupusas that were fried masa all the way through, with no filling. She did the work of a devoted member of the Church and then some, and then more. War was no time for hours of quiet contemplation, and she did not want them anyway. She would acknowledge her sins, pray for forgiveness, at another time. Sometime when it was bearable.

She avoided going back to the mountain with Padre Raúl, always found other tasks that needed to be done, but she thought of that time often. When she saw him on the street, she nodded hello and turned away. She resisted going to the mango tree, the one peaceful place she knew, in order to keep her religion.

Agnes had always known she wanted to be a nun. To cut the clutter out of life and focus on the work. She had made the decision at a young age, with the certainty with which she made all decisions. This had exempted her from considering her options, weighing the pros and cons; it was simply who she was. It had been easy for her to take her final vows at the age of twenty-four, with no knowledge of romantic intimacy. She had been so, so focused then, certain she was gaining far more than she was giving up. Agnes tried to remember that feeling, the spiritual drive that was so much more powerful than sensuality.

In spite of herself, she thought often of his body against hers, that day at the foot of the mountain. She pushed it away, along with the feeling that she was barely human anymore. She could not waver now, when things got a little difficult.

In the evenings, instead of going to the mango tree, she took to going to the small room in the house that was designated as a chapel. It was the only space for prayer after the church had been bombed. The room was barely large enough for a kneeler and two chairs situated in front of a small statue of the Virgin, a small, golden pyx containing the consecrated Eucharist, and a wooden cross affixed to the wall.

Agnes kneeled. She prayed endless rosaries, asking for strength, for faith—things that had come naturally to her, before. The face of the Virgin, which had once appeared radiant to her, was now only painted wood, stiff and unchanging. Gone was the certainty that God walked beside her, and in its place, loneliness, meaninglessness, and temptation pressed in. This was a dark night of the soul; she needed to keep believing, praying, working, and God would come back to her.

One evening, as this absence became more intolerable, her shoulders hunching and her breaths coming quicker, Sister Margaret joined her. The kneeler groaned under their combined weight. Out of the corner of her eye, Agnes saw her sister's small, tanned hands fidgeting with the blood-red beads of her own rosary. She tried to gather her thoughts, to slow her breathing and straighten her shoulders, and most of all to ignore her sister's presence; she was growing weaker, succumbing more each day to the difficulties. After a time, Agnes forced an exhale, crossed herself, and stood. Sister Margaret did the same. She caught Agnes's eye, gestured to the chairs, and asked her to sit with her a while. Agnes studied Sister's Margaret's soft blue eyes, set deeply within the fragile bones of her small face. She was so small, compared to Agnes, so breakable. Just for a moment, she would sit with her.

Shoulder to shoulder in the small chairs, Sister Margaret asked Agnes, What's wrong?

Agnes's first instinct was to snort and say, Where to begin? Look around you. But she knew Sister Margaret wasn't asking about that. She was asking about Agnes. Of course, Agnes couldn't tell her. How could she reveal the thoughts that plagued her, especially to one so delicate, who was practically on a plane back to the States?

Come back to Boston with me, Margaret said. Life doesn't have to be this difficult all the time. You'll be here when this whole town goes up in flames. You think that if you die it won't matter? There is a whole community at home that loves you. Besides, you have to be alive to do God's work.

Agnes looked away from Margaret, toward the altar.

You were going to get your master's in theology, Margaret persisted. You could still be a great educator. Return to that calling.

So Agnes said only, Can we just sit here together?

Sister Margaret nodded and took Agnes's hand in hers. Agnes could think only of the clamminess of the other woman's hands, the awkwardness of touch from someone for whom she had lost respect, but after a few moments Agnes allowed herself to find comfort in that touch, from the last remaining person in the same situation as her. The only sound was their breathing, and gradually their inhales and exhales synchronized. At least Agnes was not literally, physically alone. She still had that.

CHAPTER 8

LA VIDA ES DURA

One night as the rainy season was nearing an end, Agnes was invited to dinner at the home of María, a woman who often volunteered with Agnes. She lived on the other side of town with her parents and her two children, ages seven and nine, whom her husband had left her to raise alone when he went to the United States years ago. María was undeterred by this abandonment; she went on chatting with everyone who still lived in the community and grew tougher, as did the many other Salvadoran women in her situation. When she told Agnes about it, she said, La vida es dura, and left it at that.

It was the time of day just before the rain would come, followed by darkness. Agnes walked, carrying with her an umbrella and a large watermelon. Sweat leached from every pore in her body and combined with the humid air to make a dewy paste on her skin. A truck clattered up the street behind her and, in spite of herself, her spine clenched. It slowed as it drew close to her. Agnes continued walking and did not turn around.

Buenas, Hermana Agnes, a deep, quiet voice said.

Agnes's spine loosened and her heart quickened.

Buenas, she said to Padre Raúl.

She should have known. There had been a creaking noise that meant it was an old vehicle in need of repairs: nonmilitary.

Where are you heading? May I give you a ride?

His face shone with the healthy sweat of a body familiar with the heat.

I am going to María's home for dinner, she said.

His face became even brighter.

As am I, he said. I am glad to save you a walk.

Agnes knew she could not say no. It would be rude to him and exhausting for her if she insisted on walking. Besides, according to a new military order, soldiers could now, with impunity, do whatever they wanted to anyone they did not recognize, a previously unwritten rule made official. She climbed into the truck, a different one.

In answer to her unasked question, he told her the truck they drove to the mountain was set on fire. He went back later and found only a charred shell. Fortunately there was more than one vehicle available to him. She thought of the connections he must have, a network like an invisible spiderweb stretching across the country.

Couldn't they have traced the truck back to you? she asked.

They could have, if it were mine, he said. But the owner was already killed by the junta.

I see, she said.

He glanced at her.

You don't have a car? he asked.

I did, but it broke down, she said. I've been writing to international organizations, asking for another one to be donated.

Ah, he said.

They trundled on in silence.

You have been avoiding me, he said. I have respected your wish for distance, but we were becoming friends. Friendship is what matters most in these times; I would like it if we could have that again.

He sat so calmly, driving with his two thumbs, Agnes couldn't remember why she had felt she needed to separate herself from him. A wall was building up in her, one that she would not be able to bring down on her own. Padre Raúl was the only person who did not need her help. When she was in pain, he had comforted her, that was all. She was too tired to say no to a friend.

I would like that, she said. I am sorry for avoiding you. I suppose I was embarrassed.

Embarrassed, he said, incredulous.

I did not take my vows lightly, she said. I intend to keep them.

I did not take my vows lightly, either, he said. I do not break them unless I am certain.

Agnes sat in silence, watching the cobblestones disappear under the truck. She wondered if he had broken other vows, and if so which ones, and why.

They arrived at the Ramos home to the lively clatter of three generations of family in a too-small house made of cement. María greeted them with hugs and kisses, wearing a shirt that said in English, *Be kind to nurses*, though she spoke no English and surely didn't know what it meant. The two children, an older boy and a younger girl, wrapped their impossibly thin arms around Agnes's and Raúl's midsections. Their grandparents, mild and gray-haired, sat calmly in their chairs and shook Agnes's and Raúl's hands with their gnarled ones. The air was filled with the aroma of sweet-fatty smells of fried plantains and eggs and casamiento, beans and rice mixed together: breakfast for dinner, the meal for those who could not afford to buy anything else. Agnes announced that desayuno típico was her favorite meal.

Most of the chairs were plastic, but María seated Raúl and Agnes at well-loved wooden chairs with worn pillows on the seats. She brought Raúl and Agnes plates of food, the best and largest helpings. Even so, it was not quite enough food.

Then they each had their portion of watermelon, a juicy sliver over which everyone exclaimed, Es rica—the one compliment for food Agnes had ever heard from a Salvadoran, though it seemed genuine every time. At first, Agnes had tried to create some variety with Es deliciosa or Es sabrosa or even Es bien, but it had never been received with quite the pleasure Es rica brought.

After the meal, they sat with their hands on their bellies, relaxed and pretending they were full, drinking watered-down corn coffee. Real coffee was exported, and what little remained was too expensive, so instead corn was toasted, then mixed with a few coffee beans, if there were any to be had, and boiled in water. Agnes added heaping spoonfuls of sugar to hers and listened to the rapid exchange of Spanish. The conversation faded into María telling a story two hours long about everything her brother and sister had done when she was a girl, while her parents gently nodded off in their chairs and the children played and fought in the background.

When Raúl and Agnes left to a chorus of goodbyes, María followed them out, shutting the door behind her. The three of them stood on the narrow sidewalk, elevated several feet above the street for reasons Agnes never understood. Raúl and Agnes waited for María to speak.

I need your help, she said. I have to send my family away from here while I still can.

Where to? Agnes asked.

The mountain, María said.

You want your parents and children to live on the mountain? she asked. It's a hard life. I've seen it.

Better than here, María said. At least there they have a chance. Did you hear that the junta now says that all unrecognized inhabitants are insurgents and can be shot on sight? Who decides which inhabitants are recognized? In their eyes we are all revolutionaries. They will not stop until we are all dead.

Agnes lowered her eyes. There were bullet holes all along the house and the ones next to it.

We will help them get to the mountains, Agnes said.

I know where one community is located, Raúl said. I will take them. But I think you should have a few more weeks with them. Enjoy the time.

María grasped Agnes's hands in thanks, then Raúl's, saying, Dios te bendiga, over and over again.

As Raúl drove Agnes home, she imagined María's elderly parents in the mountains, living on beans and tortillas, sometimes walking for thirty hours at a time without stopping, or hiding in a tatú for days.

Raúl turned the radio to the classical station. It was Bach, a cello suite. She gazed out the window.

Do you miss the stars during the rainy season? she asked.

He looked to the sky, where there was nothing but clouds.

I have never seen so many stars as there are here, he said. There is too much city light in San Salvador. Yes, I miss them, but the waiting makes it so much better when the dry season finally arrives. And then by the end of the dry season I miss the greenness of the rainy season, and the relief of daily rainfall. So I don't miss the stars too much because I know I will see them again.

You have patience, Agnes said. That is not a virtue I was born with.

You seem patient to me, he said.

Agnes laughed, for the first time in weeks, or months. The corners of her mouth were stiff. He smiled.

The truck emitted an especially loud clank, followed by a hissing sound. Smoke curled out from the hood, from the exhaust pipe; it was as if they were enveloped in it. Raúl let out a slew of Spanish too quick for Agnes to understand, then slammed the breaks and pulled over. He got out of the truck and inspected underneath the hood, then came back and leaned his head in through the window.

His voice a little too calm, a little too quiet, he said, It cannot be fixed tonight. We must not linger here in the dark. We will have to walk the last few blocks. Quick as we can.

Agnes felt cold despite the heat. She gathered her things and hopped out of the truck, gripping her umbrella as if it were a sword. She fell into step beside Raúl on the narrow sidewalk. He set a brisk pace and Agnes struggled to keep up, but she could not ask him to slow down. He had sensed danger. They walked in silence down the empty street.

A moment later, he tensed almost imperceptibly and increased the pace. Then she heard it, too. Footsteps, not far behind them. How many she could not tell. It was almost impossible not to turn around but she knew she mustn't. She strained her ears. Were those military boots against the cobblestones? She chanced a glance behind her. There were several men, none wearing uniforms, but that no longer meant anything. Death squads wore plainclothes.

Just shy of a run, the adjoined houses and buildings nearly a blur, Raúl and Agnes covered the last two blocks to their homes.

The men muttered, perhaps orders. When Padre Raúl and Agnes turned the final corner to their home, the men continued walking. His shoulders sagged.

His voice still a whisper, he said, I had just fixed up the truck. There should not be anything wrong with it.

We made it, we are home, Agnes said, using the soothing tones she usually reserved for the mothers who received unwanted packages from her.

I will walk you to your door, he said.

He was the one who needed a human shield, she thought, but allowed him to take her to her door. She lingered there, hand on the wrought iron door that was like a fence or a cage, and met Raúl's gaze. He raised his eyebrows.

At least walk through the garden, she said.

Very well, he said.

He walked into her home, hands in his pockets, and she escorted him to the back of the house and into the garden.

Before he went into the clergy house, he paused and looked at her.

There's more you could do, you know, he said. If you wanted.

Such as? she asked.

Perhaps we can talk about it, he said. I will tell you

about the work I am doing and you can decide if you would like to join. You should know it is dangerous. Even talking about it.

Everything is dangerous. Look what just happened, she said.

He nodded.

I will think about it, she said.

She was too alive with nerves to answer now, though she was already burning to do more; he must have sensed it in her.

If you decide you want to know, meet me under the mango tree tomorrow evening, he said. Buenas noches, Agnes. And thank you.

I did not do anything, she said.

Sometimes your presence is all that's needed, he said, then turned on his heel and walked the few feet to the back door of his house, shoulders hunched.

Agnes went back inside and got into the shower with unheated water, and watched goose bumps pop up all over her skin. She wondered if they had been followed or if it had been coincidence; if there had been orders that somehow were called off, because she was there, an accidental human shield. She tried to remember just an hour before, when she was sipping corn coffee in a little cement house, listening to María talk and talk while everyone else hid yawns and nodded politely. She wondered how she could be so many different people in one day, and then in the shower, be a soft, vulnerable thing that no one saw, a creature without its shell. She leaned her head against the wall, sending a nearby gecko skittering, and let the water freeze her.

CHAPTER 9

TRANQUILITY AND TRUST

The next evening, Agnes waited for him on the bench. He emerged, a glimmer of a smile at the sight of her. He carried a stack of books and pamphlets.

Am I correct in interpreting your presence as interest in what I spoke of last night? he asked as he took his place next to her.

If I'm going to risk my life every day, I want it to count, she said. You are right that I am interested in doing more, but first I want to know more.

I would expect nothing less, he said. To begin: tell me what you know of liberation theology.

He placed his hands on the stack of texts between them. Her eyes flicked down to them, then back to his face. Her back went rigid.

It is a radical movement based in Marxism that risks destabilizing the authority of the Church's teachings, she said.

He smiled, an indulgence.

That's not exactly accurate, he said. May I explain?

Under other circumstances, had anyone else asked her,

she could have said no, with confidence. He sat before her, still yet bristling with energy, open and certain.

Perhaps, she said.

He raised his eyebrows.

Yes, proceed, she said.

Very good, he said. Liberation theology only has in common with Marxism the desire to empower the poor. Marx opposed religion, while liberation theology is rooted in it. But now we must cover the reasons such a philosophy is suited for this place. Latin America is the only continent of oppressed peoples who are mostly Christian.

She thought, and realized he might be correct. Almost everyone she had met in El Salvador was Christian, and everyone she had met was oppressed. From her knowledge of the rest of the continent, it seemed representative.

It is important, he continued, to distinguish the difference between underdeveloped and oppressed. An underdeveloped country would need economic stimuli to develop. An oppressed country needs to be freed. El Salvador, as you have seen, is so much more than underdeveloped; it consists of owners and slaves, and only the slaves can be the liberators. To receive assistance from an outside force would indebt the people to a new power, make them appear to be a passive element, and compromise their agency. The change has to come from the oppressed country itself.

So, as an American, I should not interfere, she said.

Agnes, eres una de las nuestras, he said.

Agnes rolled his words in her mind. *Una de las nuestras.* One of us. She had not known how much she had longed to hear those words to come, genuine, out of a Salvadoran's mouth. She had suspected, for some time now, that she was more Salvadoreña than American. She could not think of anyone she had left behind who would truly be worse off without her. She was not close with her brother, the favorite child. Her parents were gone, because of her, and they would have pushed her to do more anyway. There were plenty of sisters to do the work in Massachusetts. Here, however, she felt a part of the community in a way she never had at home. She belonged, she had a purpose. She was wanted. A smile cracked open Agnes's face before she could stop it. She waited for him to explain further, but he did not.

Why must the Church be involved in social and political change? she asked.

As he resumed his lesson, he seemed to become lighter, buoyant. He spoke of the increasing demand within the Church for action in service of others, which Latin American priests, nuns, and theologians had taken to heart. It had become clear that for the continent to be liberated, eventually violence would be necessary.

Frustration sprouted in her. She was impatient to know, to understand, even if just to prove liberation theology wrong. Catholicism was conservative, not radical. Traditional, not revolutionary. She stooped over, picked up a sturdy, long stick, and began driving it into the ground.

This could all be seen as a justification for violence—Church-sanctioned murder, she said.

It is violence that we speak out against, he said. Bishops are denouncing the institutionalized violence occurring in the impoverished areas they oversee. The focus of our struggle is justice and peace, wealth and poverty—the latter two are the subjects Jesus discussed most. One of every ten verses in the Gospels. It is true that these topics inevitably become political and economic. But since when has religion kept to its own sphere? You have gone about your life as a religious person. Does that mean there are parts of your life unaffected by your beliefs? Religion should not be hidden away when difficult subjects arise.

They spoke until well after darkness had descended and mosquitoes nipped at their elbows and ankles. She was entranced by him, the way he spoke of this theology as if it were a part of him. It was something she didn't think she could ever understand. When they parted, he handed her the stack of books as supplemental reading, and said that if she wanted to meet the next day, he would tell her what the liberationists were doing in El Salvador.

That night, as she slipped in the bed next to her one remaining sister, who had long been asleep, a Bible verse he had quoted echoed in her mind. La obra de la justicia será paz, y el servicio de la justicia, tranquilidad y confianza para siempre. The effect of righteousness will be peace, and the result of righteousness, tranquility and trust forever.

In the days and weeks to come, they met nearly every evening. He told her of the communities he and his fellow priests had formed, how they had trained leaders and awakened the campesinos with liberation theology. It showed them how to change something that was not working and make it functional. And yes, when changing things peacefully failed, they assisted the guerrilleros. Guerrilleros were the people of El Salvador, he said, and it is the role of the Church's disciples to aid the poor as they free themselves of servitude and become masters of their own fates.

The more she learned, the more restlessness stirred within her. Despite aspects of the movement that contradicted everything she had been taught about relying on the traditions of the Church, the authority of the Vatican,

Agnes could not find a better way to bring her need for action to fruition.

One evening, weeks later, he said he had taught her what she needed to know. He asked her if she had decided.

Agnes studied the dark leaves above her. Liberation theology had not sunk into her the way it had Raúl; it had been born at the same time as him, in the same land, and he had been raised with it. She wished she had a belief that came from inside of her, where she could reach inside and pull it out and know it as truly as her own breath. But they had talked for countless hours. He had walked her through the logic and the morals of it. She had analyzed the information and felt the truth of it in her experiences.

The tactics, however—she did not think she could ever support violence. And she could not give herself to a whole ideology. She had done that once, when she became a nun, and look how she failed at that, time and time again. How her prayers were met with emptiness, how her sins overwhelmed her work.

Besides, she had never intentionally acted in a way that departed from the Church before. Though it was not something she thought she would ever do, she thought of the starving children with distended bellies, the families of seven or more living in one-room mud huts, the severed heads of teenage boys on stakes, and was driven by the force within herself, so strong it overpowered her misgivings.

I cannot be a true liberation theologist or a guerrillero, she said. But I want to help more, and this is the best way I can see to do so.

She looked him directly in the eye.

The Church can never know what I am doing, she said.

It won't, he said.

CHAPTER 10

LA CONSPIRACIÓN

She began to join in his work. He hosted prayer groups as a front for revolutionary meetings, and all the while she made note of how he spoke with a quiet leadership that made others join him, so she could also do it, someday. She walked people home from these meetings, as their protection. She made more trips with him to the mountains, which went far more smoothly than their first trip together. Along the way, they stopped at various earth-floored huts in the campo, wayposts of the movement, to collect verbal messages from sharecroppers with missing teeth. Agnes and Raúl passed these messages to the people in the mountains, and while they were there, they taught and prayed, held Mass and offered sacraments.

They gathered one Thursday evening in the home of someone she did not know, in a neighborhood she knew never to go to at night. The windows were boarded up to hide their activities. Hymnals were tucked under crooked arms and placed on laps; the meeting's cover was a Vespers service. Dozens of people crowded in, mostly men, but many were joined by their wives and older children. The air thrummed with suppressed voices and ripe bodies. Having arrived early, Agnes sat in a small wooden chair in a corner of the room, sweating gently. Raúl stood beside her.

A bespectacled man went to the front of the room and stood with open arms, until the packed room gradually took note and quieted. Then he began the meeting with a speech. He was a former priest who had left the clergy to pursue guerrilla activities. He was impassioned, intense, charming to a degree that brought everyone in, which in turn made Agnes suspicious at first. But his words were poetry and they were true. He told the group that the FMLN was la conspiración, the same term that was used by the early Christians of the Roman Empire. The word contained all the power of its Latin roots. "Con," meaning "with" and "spirar," meaning "breath, spirit, inspire." Their community was created in the breath of the Spirit. He spoke of the earth and of the blood and bone of the people as if they were one. He advocated that they all leave the towns and go to the mountains where they belonged. Cities are dead, he said, and we must go where there is life, where the leaves are painted red with our blood, with justice. Entonces, sabemos socarla. Then we will know how to progress.

The man concluded his speech, was received with nods of agreement and pats on his arm and back as he sat.

One man stood. A boy still, really. It was Rafael, Tatiana's son. He shifted from one foot to the other, then the other, then the other. There was a tremor of desperation in his voice.

My brother was killed, he said. Now I myself must join either the guerrilleros or the military to survive. To join the military means a good paycheck. I could feed all my brothers and sisters with that money. It would lift them out of poverty and suffering. To join the guerrilleros is a life on the run, and almost certain death. How can I join the guerrilleros knowing all this?

Raúl stepped forward.

Fear of death will kill you faster than any gun, he said. Once you know you are ready to give your life for something, then you can think calmly, even in the most dangerous situations. Decide what you are willing to die for, and fight for it—that will keep you alive more surely than constantly trying to outrun death.

Raúl stood before them, strong and straight, as if he knew without doubt that what he said was true. She realized it must be—otherwise, how could Raúl or anyone in the movement do what they did, knowing the risks? They saw mutilated corpses every day, knowing it could be theirs tomorrow, and continued the work, seemingly unaffected.

There was a murmur of interest, agreement. Agnes looked to see Rafael's response, but his face was hidden by the undulating crowd. Raúl turned to Agnes.

It is time, he said.

He touched her elbow, guiding her to stand up.

I disagree, Agnes said, reluctant to speak again after her failed speech on the mountain.

You know everything I know, and the people listen to you. You have the makings of a great speaker in you. I know it.

Mothers, wives, and daughters listen to me. Not these men.

Only because you have not spoken to them yet, he said.

The crowd was becoming restless, murmuring, fidgeting. Raúl called them to attention. Compañeros y compañeras. He introduced Agnes as a spirited young revolutionary, new to the cause but a true Salvadoreña. With her American connections, he was sure she was an essential part of the fight for freedom.

Agnes longed to know, deep inside her, what the man who had spoken before her meant. Raúl called her one of them, but she was a New Englander, a city girl. She could not truly know what it was to not only be one of them, but one *with* them. Who was she to speak?

Raúl had already told her: the people listen to their religious leaders, they turn to us for guidance.

He was extending an arm, a gesture to hand the floor over to her. She took his place at the front and center, swallowed, stared out at the room. She had not spoken in public since college, was unaccustomed to the gazes directed at her. Some men, perhaps even many of them, sneered at the sight of her—white, a woman—and a couple of viejitos even looked ready to nod off, chests against chins. The women looked more open, skeptical but with a tinge of hope in their bodies, arms and legs uncrossed. She looked at them, many faces she recognized and loved—there was María in the back—others she did not know, all of them lacking clean water to drink, less food every day, no work, and constant fear of becoming the next example made by the military. As she took them in, she felt in the air a new energy; there was something alive in this place, more than the people themselves. It was the spirit of freedom, of undying hope, of El Salvador. This energy permeated the room, and sank into her.

She opened her mouth and began to speak. Though she had worked with Raúl to prepare a speech, what came out were unplanned words. She barely knew what she said; some force had taken over her body and mind and was speaking for her. She knew she spoke of the deep admiration she had for the Salvadoran people, how they gave her a strength she never knew she had, and how she would use that strength to continue in the struggle with them. She mentioned the peace already attempted and advocated for continued efforts to negotiate. How in the meantime, they would protect the meek among them. This is what Christianity looks like, she said, her voice rising to the rafters and taking her audience with her. People oppressed, meeting in secret, fighting for the rights of the poor. She thumped a fist against her chest. We know what's right, in here, she said.

When she finished speaking, she did not know how long she had addressed the room. Her hands, which had been gesticulating, floated to her sides. She was panting and underneath her arms there was dampness.

She looked around the room—what would the reaction be? Everyone was still. She waited for anything, a smile, a frown. Next to her, Raúl was frozen. His hair, which was growing long, hung in a wavy curtain around his face. If Agnes didn't know better, she would have thought his expression was one of awe. His body leaned toward her, as a flower leans to the sun.

At last, his face and body released from their fixed position and he took one step to stand before her. As if waiting for him, the rest of the group stood, enclosed around her. People touched her, hugged her, abuzz with kind words. More than one person, their eyes shining, admired what they called her energy and zeal. As they pressed against her, engulfed her, she lost the sense of herself, was swept up in the collective energy of the room. Oneness.

After her, several others spoke and she stood in the back, listening with rapt attention. Then they sipped corn coffee and discussed their plans. Together, they could do anything.

Chapter 11

Farabundo Martí National Liberation Front

Agnes was on the mountain again. She had volunteered to come with Raúl on a trip to provide religious services to the people in the mountains. She hoped to find Elisa, perhaps Lito, though she knew that of the many hiding deep in the mountain's belly, she was unlikely to encounter them.

This time, she was prepared, with army-green clothing and thick-soled boots. On her back was a light pack containing a vial of holy water and just enough supplies to last twenty-four hours.

She and Raúl and several men—former farmers who had come along to protect them—hiked, mostly in silence, for what Agnes estimated was three hours. She tried not to look at the oversize guns they carried. She wanted to ask if it was really necessary for a priest and a nun to be under armed guard, but she knew it would be pointless.

When at last they reached the site, she only knew because the others stopped walking, fetched water and cloths to wipe their faces. There was nothing here, only tall maquilishuat trees with their dark, leathery leaves, and yucca trees growing bell-shaped izotes. As she watched, however, men emerged, from the trees, the bushes, the ground. Some wore leaves and branches attached to their clothes. She was witnessing the power of guerrilla tactics. They were chameleons, blending in seamlessly with their surroundings. She looked around and saw what she'd missed before: earth-colored hammocks, dusty green packs, dirty faces.

They gathered around the newcomers, greeting them, surveying them. Agnes had expected typical Salvadoran warmth from them, a lightheartedness even in the darkest times, but she realized they were warriors who never knew when battle would be upon them; they had no room to let down their guard. Agnes had learned that at all times they carried their weapons, wore their shoes, were ready to fight without a moment's notice. She could not imagine living like that for years on end—though she realized that, in a way, she had been.

As they began their work, giving last rites to the gravely injured, who were hanging in blankets suspended between two long sticks, she noticed how young many of them looked. Beneath the dirt, they were children, she was almost certain of it. She felt a nearly uncontrollable urge to lick her thumb and scrub their faces clean. Were they sixteen, fourteen, twelve? Some looked like they had not begun puberty. They carried rifles that were larger than them—rifles stolen, she knew, from the military.

Raúl administered the blessings and a brief Mass. Just before the Eucharist was brought out, distant booms rattled the ground, their bodies. Everyone tensed, cocked their heads to listen.

Air bombs, one guerrillero said.

On the west side of the mountain, said another. We are on the east. Go on, Padre.

And they continued the Mass through the sounds and the vibrations, ignoring them as if it were normal. It *was* normal.

After the ceremony, the group dispersed into so many people getting back to work. Agnes helped Raúl pack up the chalice, host box, and altar cloth.

I think I'm losing my mind, she said. I think I am seeing children. Child soldiers.

Raúl gave her a sidelong glance.

Children here are recruited very young, he said. There are child soldiers on both sides. The army conducts mass conscriptions from buses, schools, football grounds. If their families resist, they are killed. The only way to avoid that is to come here, where the FMLN can care for them. It is their war, too.

She stared at him.

That's all? she said. How do we work on the same side as an organization that uses children to fight their war?

La guerra es así, he said. We are not angels versus demons in this. No one joins the guerrilleros by choice; it is the last chance for survival for every one of these boys.

He gestured at the soldiers, cleaning their weapons, eating foraged roots, disappearing back into the foliage.

Amor de vida, he said. If you have the possibility to save your life, you take it. Even if that means picking up a gun.

It's wrong, she said.

He bowed his head for a moment, then looked back at her.

Yes it is, he said simply.

What else is the FMLN doing? she asked.

You do not want to know, he said. I do not even know. What you and I are doing, however—there is nothing wrong with celebrating Mass with people who are going to be here anyway.

She swallowed the bile that rose to her throat.

We have to fight this, she said. So these children have to flee to the mountains—many families do the same. It does not mean they need to fight.

You are right, he said.

They stood, facing each other. No solution rose between them.

He looked tired. An instinct told her to wrap him in her arms; she felt herself swaying toward him and forced herself to sway back. She took a step away to cover the movement.

As they descended the mountain, side by side, their gaits aligned. They had spent so much time together in the last weeks—months now—that she knew his movements as well as her own.

She took in the darkened curves of the mountain, the babbling of the streams; she felt the air, always alive, always warm as a human body.

I understand now, she said, what you and your people have always known. The mountain is the root of all things Salvadoran.

He smiled, bumped his shoulder against hers, a welcome.

C H A P T E R 12

W E B E L O N G T O D E A T H

Agnes's letters had paid off. She now had, donated from Catholic Charities, a dusty blue Jeep. She drove, with Raúl in the passenger seat, María's family crammed into the back, on the way back to the mountain, which was becoming a second home to her. Though she fought it, tried not to let anyone see it, she felt a sense of pride over the car. She had been without a vehicle for a year. Once, subconsciously, she stroked the steering wheel.

What a lovely Monte Carlo you have, Raúl said.

She shot him a glance. He grinned.

It is nothing, she said.

A car is everything, he said.

In the rearview mirror, she saw the older couple staring out the window as if taking in the last sights they'd ever see. Squished between them, the two children took turns pinching each other, the situation escalating until the younger child let out a great yelp. Their grandmother inter-vened with a solid scolding, and hauled the seven-year-old onto her lap.

· · ·

69

When they made it to the civilian camp some hours later—both grandparents and children having somehow kept up on the long walk without complaint—they were welcomed warmly. The whole camp, dozens of people at work and rest, left their activities to swarm the newcomers: coffee was pressed into their hands, greetings of ¡Compas! ¡Bienvenidos! all around. María's family was swept off to be introduced to the whole camp.

Agnes spotted Lito and made her way toward him. After a quick greeting, she asked him if he had seen Elisa.

He shook his head, his eyes dark.

No, Hermana, Lito said. We did not see her again after that day.

He stabbed the heel of his rifle into the grassy earth below.

Agnes felt a sinking, a pull to the ground. What she had felt that first time leaving the mountain. She fought it, cast around for something to do.

There was a group of a half dozen small children, running around barefoot. They all carried sticks, aimed them at each other and made gunshot noises. The other children fell down, mimicking death. They took turns ambushing each other.

Agnes made her way over to them. They dropped their makeshift weapons and descended upon her, pulling at her hands, chattering in such quick Spanish she could not understand them. She sat on a stump and gathered them around, hearing their stories, admiring their flower wreaths, one of which was bestowed upon her.

Children had been excellent for practicing Spanish when she first arrived. Everything was novel to them, so nothing was odd, not even her broken words. Though she had taught children in Boston and had thought it a fine enough task, she felt at home with them here.

Tell me, niños, she said. What do you know about the war?

The war is how we're going to get freedom, a boy said. And justice. For our families who were killed in the massacre.

He spoke casually while he played with the flowers in Agnes's hair, as if he had said these things many times before.

Yes, the grown-ups are fighting very hard, Agnes said. They hope you will have a better life when you grow up.

We are going to fight, too, a girl said. I'm joining as soon as I'm twelve.

The others nodded eagerly; so were they. Agnes wished she were more surprised. She steeled herself.

Who is making you do that? Agnes said.

The girl puffed up her chest, not yet starting to bud.

No one, she said. I decided. I can read and write, too, so I can be a messenger. Or I can go to Morazán and help with the radio. That's what my sister did.

What about school? Agnes said. Don't you want to learn to read and write even better? Then you can do anything when you grow up. All kinds of important things.

The girl shrugged. She picked up her stick, aimed it at another child, and they were off once again. Not playing, Agnes realized, but practicing. María's children ran over to join them.

The sinking feeling threatened to return, but Agnes resisted. There was always something to do.

. . .

Driving in El Salvador was different from driving in the States. It was a dance with no choreography. At first she did not understand how anyone avoided getting into an accident every day, zipping around and through the tiniest spaces, slowing just in time to avoid collisions with others who were doing the same. Drivers were more aware, more aggressive but also more responsive. But when she had grown used to it, she found she liked the gliding give and take.

As they approached home, the sky turning from orange to twilight blue, Agnes thought, hard.

I feel that I have sent María's children off to become combatants, she said. They won't have a choice in it. They won't know it, but they won't have a choice. It is the only option for them there.

Raúl looked up from studying his palms. He nodded.

There are refugee camps in Nicaragua and Honduras, she said. Why aren't families and children going there?

Only so many refugees are accepted, he said. And it is difficult to do all the paperwork, especially for those who do not know how to read. But mostly they would not want to leave their land. Their people.

And the refugee camps here in El Salvador? she said.

The conditions are bad, he said. And the camps are often raided by the military. People can disappear from there just as easily as anywhere else.

She slowed for a herd of cattle to amble across past the car, their protruding bones so sharp they looked as if they could cut through the cows' hide. She chewed on all the knowledge she had, all the people she had met in her six years here.

What if there were a place children could go that was separate from the war? Agnes said. They could learn and play and be children. It would still be in the mountains, where it was safe, but hidden from both the guerrilleros and the military. A true sanctuary.

Secret boarding school in the mountains? Raúl said, a glimmer in his eye.

Agnes almost smiled. Yes, she said.

It is a nice thought, but who would care for the children? Raúl said.

I would, she said, putting the full force of herself behind her words. Tatiana, maybe. María. Any number of women who want to keep their children safe.

He contemplated her for a moment.

How can I help? he asked.

CHAPTER 13

THE ONES WHO LIVED

It was well into the dry season, when the weather was most comfortable and the mountains had just started to brown, that Agnes's last sister left. Agnes bade Margaret goodbye, kissed her, and told her to write often. Agnes dared not cry. In her sister's eyes was an apology she ignored.

That night, the noises of the now-empty house, the scratching of rats and the near-silent swooping of the bats, were amplified. A spider on the wall watched her, its brown legs angular and menacing. It was too big to kill with a shoe and besides, she had already had too much of death. When she finally dozed off, images of torn bodies hovered before her, and she jerked awake.

It was her parents' bodies in a ruined vehicle, still and bleeding, that she saw now.

The prayers she uttered were empty words against the darkness. Still, she prayed until dawn.

Agnes went on with her duties, sleep or no sleep. Almost always no sleep. She taught at the makeshift school with the same vigor as always, trying her best to teach them to read and write in the midst of a war, even when her head felt alternately heavy as a dumbbell and light as cotton. It was not the children's fault she was tired, so they would not suffer for it. Now, though, she was also recruiting them for her refuge in the mountains.

She wrote letters, requesting funds for the school, to international aid organizations and wealthy individuals in Europe and the States, double-checking them for her own fatigue-ridden errors and rewriting them. Words, at times, ceased to make sense to her. So far, there had only been polite declines, citing the cost, the underground nature of the program. For each rejection she received, she sent five more letters.

There was another head on a spike, which she brought to a mother. She sometimes stumbled over her own feet. She had never been clumsy before.

At night, she listened for the sounds of soldiers' boots outside her door. Perhaps they would come for her now that she was alone. Any moment they would enter her home, any moment bombs would destroy this little house with her inside it. Once, she heard it happening to another house.

One night, as she lay listening to the swoop of bat's wings above her, she heard a flurry of activity in one of the homes that adjoined hers. Objects scraped floors, feet shuffled. Agnes rose and went to the window. A full moon hung in the sky. She watched three hunched figures carrying one bag each, hurrying down the street. Then they were out of sight.

She got back into bed, the new silence from next door pressing in on her. The spider was closer tonight—she could have reached out and touched it. The rats scratched inside the wall behind her head. Her breath became shorter and shorter, she could not breathe, surely she would die soon—and she could bear it no longer.

She rose from her cot and fled outside in her nightgown, past the mango tree, to the back door of the clergy house. She banged on the door, her last prayer that he would answer.

Almost immediately, he did, and when he saw her face, he took her in his arms. He held her thundering heart against his, until the beats slowed into the same steady rhythm.

If there was a God, he was not here. If there was a God, he had brought them together, to bring each other comfort and love.

She looked up at him and his eyes held the warmth she had not known she had always been looking for.

A father once told me, if you don't love each other, you are muerto viviente, she said, and kissed him.

They were the ones who stayed, the ones who fought, the ones who lived.

He lay her down on her cot and gazed upon her. Her hair spread out over the pillow, her body loose under her nightgown, unbound from the trappings of daytime clothing. She was conscious of her breasts falling to either side of her, something no man had seen before. She exhaled and he closed his eyes, tipping his head to hers.

They were both inexperienced; it was clear in their fumbling fingers, their long pauses. Only their complete inability to restrain themselves a moment longer kept them moving forward. Tentatively, she pulled off his shirt. He untied the string of her nightgown and pulled it over her head. And then his pants were off and he was on top of her, his weight a comfort. He gripped her waist, her hips, and they were sinning but she was certain it was a miracle. He paused to look into her eyes again and she looked into his and she was safe. She pulled at his neck to bring him closer and they were together until the end of the world. Together, they could survive.

CHAPTER 14

THE BEGINNING

She was a sinner and she knew that objectively, but her heart was lighter than it had been in six years, or ten years, or perhaps ever. If she had not become a nun and he had not become a priest, they would never have met, so she could regret nothing. She had become a nun to help in real ways, only to find herself handing out bandages. With Raúl, there was so much more. It was only the beginning.

They lay together late into the night, whispering about all the things they would do, now that they were together. For the first time since she had arrived in El Salvador, Agnes felt forgiven. Perhaps someday she would find the words to tell him what she needed forgiving for. She would tell him about her parents.

Her body crooked into his, every possible part of them touching despite the heat, Agnes watched the opal glow of her hands in the night contrast with Raúl's, which were like velvet, absorbing light.

Just before dawn, before the other priest would notice his absence, Raúl returned to the clergy house. He left her with a tender brush of the lips on her hand, and, as he walked away, held her fingers until their arms were stretched.

She hadn't slept, but she was full of energy. She stayed in the house all morning because she did not want to encounter anything that would take away this feeling that she was alive, and nearly everything out there was a new horror. Instead, listening to the morning strings hour on the radio, she tidied up around the house. Previously, the other sisters did the housekeeping, since Agnes was always out, doing other things. Dirt accrued quickly here, and already, the house was covered in filth. She swept up the leaves from the courtyard, then washed all the clothes and linens in the house and hung them up to dry, humming along to the music. One of the best parts of Salvadoran living was the lack of distinction between inside and outside. The bathroom and stone basin for clothes washing were outside in a covered area, but even in the bedroom and kitchen the doors were almost always open, and the space between the A-line roof and the wall was open to the luscious air, its smell of ripe fruit and sun-baked plants.

How had she never noticed the brilliant colors of the house before? The greens and yellows of the adobe walls were irresistibly cheerful. Birds, which made her think of Raúl, twittered above her in agreement.

The beauty of this place struck her, shaped itself into words—words that would compel anyone who read to understand. To provide the funding she sought to create safety in this magical place. She sat at the table and wrote, fast and hard, requesting funds for the children's refuge in the mountains.

The paper tore. She put the pen down.

This was not the way to share her words.

Soon, she had made her way to the one working pay phone in the town square. She shut herself inside it and, as the cramped space turned into a sauna, she called all the international aid organizations in her address book. She raised her voice, she gesticulated; the people walking by stared at her, most likely thinking the poor American nun had finally gone mad. Perhaps she had; but if this was madness, she wished she had lost her mind sooner.

Sometimes she only got through to a secretary or an assistant. It did not matter; they heard her speech just the same, with instructions to pass the message on to their superiors. Once, Agnes did speak to the grant administrator of an organization based in Belgium. At last, she was speaking to the person who could do something. She summoned up all the passion she had, and explained her idea to him.

I envision this organization to be school and orphanage and adoption agency, she said. A refuge for the children of war, that they become more than that. But the community cannot create this place on its own. I implore you: for this safe haven to exist, we need your help.

The man, a Mr. De Smet, listened, and even seemed to be taking notes.

I thank you for your heartfelt query, he said, his voice even and dry. It is clear that if anyone can do this, it is you. I will speak with the board and argue your case.

She thanked him vehemently and hung up the phone. The funding would happen; Agnes had never been more sure of anything.

Since she was already close to the market, she stopped there, and all the fruit looked fresher than usual, perfectly ripe. She filled her mesh bag with marañones, caimitos, pipianes, jocotes. As she was leaving the stalls, she encountered María, who greeted her and said, Hermana Agnes, you look brighter today. Agnes beamed at María. This war would be over someday and these people would heal, and she and Raúl would be here for it.

Darkness was beginning to fall as she returned home and looked out at the garden. Raúl was already there. She walked out to meet him. He heard her and turned to watch her coming. She felt suddenly unsure of what she usually did with her hands, which were sweating slightly. She wished her skirt had pockets to put them in. Agnes sat down next to him.

I suppose we should talk, she said.

About what? he said.

She felt a swooping, as if she had missed a step on the stairs. Had it not mattered to him? Then he grinned. They leaned toward each other.

I was happy today, Raúl said. Truly, unequivocally happy. It has been years since I have had that feeling.

Her insides felt as if they were on fire, both a pleasant and an unpleasant sensation.

Me, too, she said, more hesitantly.

You are worried? he said. About your vows?

Agnes considered.

I thought I would be, she said. But I have not had room for worry today. I know that will come. Guilt, too. But I cannot help but feel that we were brought together. It is the only meaning I can find in all of this. And you? Are you worried?

Traditions are good to a point, but it is time to break

with some of them, he said. People who love each other are not meant to be apart.

She allowed herself to study the lines and curves of his face, just for a moment. His eyebrows knitting together, his eyes warm, as they had been the night before. She looked away from him.

I don't know, Raúl, she said. It is so easy to say, in this moment, that this is right and good. But I have gone my whole life knowing what is right and what is not—how can I change my mind now at the first temptation?

We do not have to decide anything, he said. Perhaps we can simply spend time together, as the friends we have been?

Something she could definitively answer. She said yes.

Between them, on the slats of the bench, their hands found each other.

CHAPTER 15

A SECRET PLACE

The baby next door made loud, indiscriminate sounds. In response, the mother sporadically yelled, Pepe, in a habitual way that neither got his attention nor effectively scolded him. After six years, Agnes could almost always ignore the sounds of neighbors and she consciously did so now.

She sat at the little table in the morning shade of her courtyard to write and respond to letters. In her ever-growing stack of mail, now mostly circulated through the underground, a rare letter had made it through regular mail. It was filthy and worn, and had been postmarked from Massachusetts several weeks prior. Perhaps it was a letter from her brother. She opened it and recognized her Mother Superior's handwriting.

Dear Sister Agnes,

I have gotten word of your recent activities and must say that I am disappointed, and more than that, I'm concerned. Not only are you alone there and unprotected, but you are in dangerous territory that is well outside the purview of our order. You must cease your activities and come home at once or risk losing your place as a member of the clergy. We will decide on your penance and new placement once you have returned.

Please let us know as soon as you can reach a phone when you will arrive and we will arrange to pick you up at the airport. We will be praying for your safe and prompt return.

Your sister in Christ,
Mother Josephine

Agnes read the letter once, set it aside, and began sorting through the rest of the mail. It no longer mattered what her order or her Church asked of her. She felt a call greater than theirs. She felt that she had only now discovered it after hiding behind conformity her whole life. Conformity was another word for safety, and she was not alive if she was not doing something worth dying for. If she immersed herself in this work fully, for a few moments at a time she could shed the feeling she had had since arriving in El Salvador, in fact since her earliest memory of life: that she wasn't doing enough. And, despite what Mother Superior said, she was less alone than ever, most of the time.

Shuffling through the stack of mail, she stumbled upon another letter that had come through the regular mail. It was from Mr. De Smet, from the Belgian organization. She ripped it open, hands shaking, and found a letter.

And a check. Her hands began to shake.

That evening, she brought the letter to the mango tree and held out the letter to him. He beamed at her. And then they were both laughing.

It was not difficult to enlist María to help in the creation of the sanctuary. Tatiana, whose son Rafael had just joined the military, eagerly agreed—she had four young children who might still be protected from a life of violence. A few trusted others joined, and they formed a small crew. Agnes searched the mountains and hills across the region until she found a place so remote that no one ever visited, guerrillero or soldier.

The day they were to break ground, they set off for the mountains with tools but no materials. They would build with what was around them: wood, mud, and branches.

When they arrived, they all stopped for a moment to survey the clearing she had chosen. It was midmorning, the time of day in El Salvador that Agnes thought was most beautiful: the air a gentle caress, the sun cheerful, not glaring. A stream trickled past a meadow. Great hills rose up on all sides, cocooning the space in a small valley. The others looked at Agnes with shining eyes and clasped her hands in theirs.

Agnes assigned everyone tasks, supervising and answering questions. They started with the construction of humble facilities: a wooden building big enough for twenty children to sleep in, an outdoor classroom, and a kitchen, complete with a firepit, metate, and comal.

This, Agnes thought, was true happiness.

When everyone was intent on their tasks, she went over to the shelter, not too close to where Raúl was working, but with him in her line of sight. His skin was covered in a light glow, his eyes bright, hair mussed. Agnes allowed herself a moment to admire him, then she picked up a machete and got to work, cutting branches down to size to make a thatched roof.

They worked until it was too dark to see, then they put

down their tools and spread out the thin sheets of plastic on which they would sleep. Blisters, red and angry, spread across the palms and pads of Agnes's hands. Her back, her arms, her shoulders, protested when she moved. She was strong, but unaccustomed to manual labor—so she would grow accustomed. Soon, calluses would form and muscles would develop. There was much more work ahead of her.

Tatiana began preparing beans and tortillas for dinner. Raúl and Agnes wandered to a guayaba tree nearby. Their hands rustled through the small green leaves in the hopes of finding a ripe fruit or two, rare as it was this time of year. Someone, a man Raúl had recruited, sang the Internationale, the anthem of the guerrilleros, his voice low and sweet. María joined in, off-key but full of enthusiasm. Someone else joined in with a fiddle and Agnes looked back to see Tatiana taking a break from cooking to dance the cumbia. It was a true celebration.

When Agnes finally stepped away from the tree, giving up on finding any fruit, she noticed that fireflies were popping out—hundreds of them, then thousands, bright as stars, and dancing. They flickered on and off in a symphony of light, illuminating the jungle around them. It was impossible; she couldn't have imagined there would be so many, all at once, that she could see them and contain such a sight within her.

Fireflies, she said.

Luciérnagas, he said.

She leaned her head back to take them all in.

Chapter 16

Chalatenango heroico

She was back at home, under the mango tree. She and Raúl had agreed to meet there, though it hardly needed saying anymore. While she waited, she tried to pray, then abandoned the attempt. Instead, she replayed all her memories of him. Raúl pointing out brilliantly colored birds to her, Raúl showing her how to find a ripe mango among the dense foliage and green buds, Raúl listening to her confessions every evening, Raúl holding her in the dark, his breath against her ear.

Perhaps he was not coming. Perhaps he had begun to regret after all. She should regret, too. It was a sin; just because she did not feel God did not mean He was not there, watching them, judging them. Was this worth hell?

But she thought of Raúl's lips on her neck and all thoughts of regret and hell vanished.

Dusk grew to dark and at last she went to the clergy house and, without thinking, knocked on the door. She needed to see Raúl, would come up with a legitimate reason to be knocking. There was no answer.

· · ·

That night, she stared at the crucifix on the wall for hours. She rolled onto her side and imagined Raúl's arms wrapped around her. Her eyes were wide open the whole night.

The next day, she went again to the clergy house and knocked. Another priest answered the door. His face was ashen.

The question on her lips died. Instead she asked, What has happened?

Padre Raúl has at last been found by the death squad, he said. They assassinated him yesterday.

EPILOGUE

MUERTO VIVIENTE

2016

The leaves of the mango tree rustle in a slight breeze. They beckon Agnes. She decides she will sit on the bench, even if the volunteer is already there; she walks over and tells the girl to sit up, put her legs down, so there's room for Agnes to sit. The bench, old and rickety, groans under the weight of her large frame. She speaks with the girl about the shareholder documentation and errands in the campo. Nonessential tasks. She is only staying a few months, and one must stay for decades to do what Agnes does. The girl nods obediently. When Agnes is done and getting up to go, the girl stops her with a question.

"Sister Agnes, will you tell me what it was like when you came here? What it was like during the war?"

Agnes is startled. She turns to the girl, stiffly. Of all the volunteers who have stayed here, none have truly asked. Agnes makes sure to be too unapproachable, closed off, busy, for people to bother her with questions they all know she won't really answer. But this girl is looking at her with attentive eyes—blank, green like a lagoon—that make it clear that she would listen, and will not stop asking until she hears the truth.

Agnes could go into the kitchen and pour two glasses of jugo de jamaica. She could sit on the bench with the girl, and as the morning gives way to the heat of the day, at last she could speak. Maybe she would stop waking up in the night with that pressure on her chest, stopping her breath.

But the memories are not to be shared. She carries them with her, replays them daily, remembers and memorizes them. They are hers to keep, and hers alone. She hasn't even gone to Confession in three decades.

The volunteer's blank eyes are still fixed on Agnes.

"When someone was killed and their head was put on a spike in the park, I was the one who brought the head to the murdered person's family. I brought provisions to the people hiding in the mountains. There were many things that only I could do as a member of the Church. I had to advocate for these people. I still have to advocate for them."

"Can't they advocate for themselves?"

"Of course they can. I do it because I have to, not because they need me to."

She sees the girl opening her mouth, confused, preparing another question, but Agnes says, "That's enough." Enough of talking about herself. She goes back into the house.

On her way out, Agnes checks the girl's bedroom, which had once been shared by three of her sisters. Their cots all in a row, the three of them shivering in fear. The girl has left the light on again, wasting electricity. Agnes snaps, her body and mind possessed. She is not aware of what she does.

There is a swell, an explosion, a tearing inside her. It is dark.

When she returns to her body, heart pounding in her ears, her throat feels raw—an echo telling her she had spoken, perhaps shouted, words that came out like daggers, resounding through the house and into the garden.

Before the girl, now shivering in the doorway, can sputter a reply, Agnes flips the switch off and says "I'll be back tonight" as she leaves the house.

***

She speeds down the dirt road in her SUV, tires grinding over rocks, muttering to herself about the light the girl left on, the exorbitant electricity bill Agnes is sure to receive. Only a herd of cattle, just as emaciated as they were thirty years ago, slows her down.

She drives first to the mountain, to the place she found all those years ago that was both far and close, safe but still home, for the children. It has grown and prospered over the decades. La Academia de Luciérnagas. Firefly Academy.

She stands at the edge of the property, watching the children at play, the sounds of classes in session through open windows.

The secretary emerges from the main building and rushes over to Agnes, out of place in the jungle with her business casual attire. They walk the grounds and discuss the two adoptions going through this week: one child going to a family in Aguilares and the other in Apopa.

"Apopa is a little far, but that's okay," Agnes says.

The secretary nods eagerly.

Next Agnes drives out to the commemorative ceremony several villages away. It is the anniversary of one of the biggest massacres that occurred during the war, and she has been asked to speak.

The war is long over, a treaty signed, but if there was improvement in the lives of the poor, it was nominal. In the campo, there is still no electricity. Bathrooms are ditches. Unclean water means high infant mortality rates. Universal health care means waiting in line for hours to receive the one medication available, regardless of the complaint. Both sides had lost, in a way, and all she could do was move on, on the outside if not the inside.

It seemed that the Church had not known enough of her activities to ensure her expulsion, and the Sisters of Charity were reluctant to lose their members. She stayed because she had no one to leave the order for, and it was the only life she knew.

She arrives at the event to find an enormous potluck with mysterious purple meats, tamales, pupusas that are now stuffed with pork and cheese. There is a slideshow of photos from the massacre, bodies strewn across the streets in impossible positions. Agnes does not look.

People walking around with shrapnel still in their bodies laugh and tease one another, draped in hammocks and nestled in lawn chairs, appearing to be at peace. This irritates her.

The blood mixing into the dirt is gone, but Agnes can still see it. It is yesterday, for her. The war is never over.

"Hermana Agnes." A cheerful voice emerges from the crowd. It is María, who stands by Agnes after all these years. If Agnes had friends, María would be one. "¿Cómo estás?" she asks.

"My back hurts, you know how it goes."

"It's like I keep telling you, Hermana: You have to get a new mattress. Yours is thirty years old already."

"More than that," says Agnes. But it is the same bed she once shared with Raúl. She must keep it. The physical ache is a much more bearable way to be in pain anyway.

"And when do you go to the oncologist," María gestures to her own forehead, "for the spots?"

"Soon, next time I go to the States. If they're malignant, I'll be dead in six months so it won't matter anyway."

"If it is cancer, will you stay in the States?" María asks, a light touch to Agnes's wrist.

"No. I tried that once, right after the war, remember? It's not my home anymore; they couldn't handle me so they sent me back!" She barks the joke, but María doesn't laugh. It's not truly a joke anyway. She's happy to die here, in El Salvador. The short time she'd spent in the States after the war had been uncomfortable. She'd felt wrong there, out of place in a country with a middle class and people who complained about working forty hours a week, when all she had was her work. Not to mention the many people, her Mother Superior, her brother, her sisters, who'd seen the change in her, the new harshness in her personality and the tendency to become upset and do things she didn't remember. They had tried to get her to go to therapy—but they never considered that maybe she doesn't want to heal.

She knows that she should now ask María how she's doing, inquire after her children and her mother's hip, but if she did, they would be there another hour as María talked on and on. Instead, she asks María to take her to the stage so she can prepare for her speech. She stopped caring about people's opinions of her long ago. It is freeing to have one less thing to worry about, even though she is aware she often hurts the feelings of those who don't know her well.

But María knows her, and understands. In a way, Agnes is sure María appreciates that Agnes is the only one who can shut her up.

After she finishes her speech, a family approaches and asks her to perform the last rites for their dying patriarch. She follows them to the one-room hut, to a man not much older than her. He lies in bed, so still he doesn't appear to breathe. Agnes might have wondered if he was already dead, but she knows what death looks like.

She did not see Raúl that day. She knew that he had been shot more than once. His body, which had loved and held her, had been ripped apart without her there to protect him. They'd brought him back to the house, put his body on a bed not fifty feet away from the bench under the mango tree. But she could not show her grief to anyone; she could not ask to see him and reveal the full weight of her grief, not when they were supposed to be acquaintances and colleagues, nothing more.

This man, no, he is not dead yet. And when he does die, it will be peaceful, natural. She whispers his last rites. It is the only time that day in which she feels calm. Every last rite is for Raúl.

As she rises to leave, he asks her to give him a kiss. She obliges, and demands one in return. He presses his dry lips against her cheek, then crosses his arms over his sunken chest as if he knows.

Outside, she tells someone to bring her a beer. Suprema, she only drinks Suprema. In this part of El Salvador, there are three types of beer, which taste respectively like urine, like bread, and like water. After thirty years, the latter is the only one whose taste she has not grown sick of.

On the drive, she cracks open the beer and takes a sip.

At home, she carries the beer out to the garden with her and sits on the bench under the mango tree, which the girl has finally vacated. The whole garden is now covered by the tree's canopy. Her bones ache sitting on those broken slats, but she barely notices. A bang; she jumps. Fireworks have gone off down the street, a remnant for the celebration of the town's patron saint.

It is February and the winds come in from the lake that borders the property, bringing the prophecy of rain. She whispers into the wind, telling Raúl about his country, how it is slowly being put back together, growing into something new, how much more there is to be done. Of the man dying a death of peace. She finishes her beer and wonders when it will at last be her turn.

She glances up at the branches of the tree above her. There, waiting for her, is the first ripe mango of the season.

Author's Note

When I was a recent college graduate, I spent four months in a town in El Salvador that was deeply affected by the war, and in turn it deeply affected me. I worked for an American nun who had come to El Salvador during the war and then stayed on permanently to continue her work. I lived in her house, which was the same one she'd lived in since the war, and she told me brief and brutal stories of the war.

In addition to the nun's stories, I listened to other people who had been alive during the war. They were open to telling my fellow American volunteers and me some of the worst stories I've ever heard. I could not imagine losing my entire family, or hiding in the mountains for twelve years, or being tortured and violated. Yet the people I met told their stories with a bravery and a peace I could not understand.

I first had the idea for this story while I was still in El Salvador, and even began to write a version of it as a full-length novel upon returning. But I wasn't ready—and besides, who was I to tell this story?—so I tucked it away in the back of my mind. It reemerged seven years later, demanding to be told. I decided to tell this story with a focus on language and beauty, and in the smaller dose of a novella, so that it would not be too devastating to tell or to read.

This story is fictional and true. The Salvadoran Civil War occurred from 1980 through 1992. The United States government really did support massacre after massacre and condoned the rape and murder of both Salvadoran and American citizens. Nuns really did deliver severed heads to mothers. This much and far more occurred, yet ask almost any North American today about the Salvadoran Civil War, and there are two responses, depending on age: I don't know anything about it, and Ah, yes, I sort of remember that being in the news years ago. For those interested in learning more about El Salvador and this war, I recommend *Unforgetting* by Roberto Lovato and *What You Have Heard is True* by Carolyn Forché.

I will never be able to understand what the Salvadoran people went through, but I felt compelled to capture a small part of it on the page, to share with an American audience some version of what the people I met were so generous and brave to share with me. This story is for the people who stayed, at enormous cost to themselves, and whose staying made all the difference.

Shannon St. Hilaire is fascinated by forgotten microcosms and the complex women who lived through them. She spends just about all her time reading and writing stories about them. Also, traveling, cat-owning, and finding cottages in forests.

If you enjoyed *The Ones Who Stayed*, please leave a review on Goodreads, Amazon, or your favorite platform.

Follow Shannon St. Hilaire on Substack for sneak peeks, book recommendations, and updates on her writing.